A Sentimental Journey

Planes, Trains and Two-Star Hotels

To Dean + Mary ~
Happy Journey...
Jim Kennison

A Sentimental Journey

Planes, Trains and Two-Star Hotels

By

Jim Kennison

Bottom of the Hill Publishing
Memphis, TN
www.BottomoftheHillPublishing.com

Printed in the United States of America
ISBN: 978-1-61203-092-0

10 9 8 7 6 5 4 3 2

ABOUT THE AUTHOR

Born into an economically-challenged family in rural southern Indiana, Jim Kennison moved at a young age with his parents and three siblings to the rolling hills of central Kentucky. Although both his parents left public school after the seventh grade to find work, they were determined their four children would attend college. Each did, with all receiving advanced degrees. Jim Kennison holds a doctorate from the University of Kentucky.

Following a professional career in higher education teaching and administration in the states of New Jersey, New York, Washington and Oregon, Jim and his wife Elletta now live in their beach home on the central Oregon coast.

This is Jim Kennison's first novel for Bottom of the Hill Publishing. Other novels include Letters from a Bounty Hunter (Outskirts Press), Big Trouble in a Small Town (Avalon Books), and the soon to be released, Heartbreak Trail to Pueblo (Avalon Books). In addition to his novels, he has numerous short stories and poems to his credit, including The Stranger in Rail Camp Seven which is one of the stories in the recently published TRAILS WEST... an Anthology of Western Lore (Bottom of the Hill Publishing).

Cover photograph on A Sentimental Journey was taken by the author, Jim Kennison on one of his several European trips.

Acknowledgements

During our many trips to Europe, my wife Elletta has kept journals chronicling our adventures as we visited capitals, cities, towns and villages. The reflections of places and events in these journals have given me insights for writing this story.

I also want to acknowledge authors of various travel books, especially editions of Lonely Planet Publications and Rick Steves' guidebooks for providing supplemental information.

Special thanks to Marianne Reynolds for her helpful input.

Table of Contents

CHAPTER ONE

As his scheduled nonstop flight to London sat idling at the San Francisco departure gate, the drone of the jet engines provided a soothing offset to the tortured thoughts filling Bryce Gibson's mind. Although it had been more than a year since the death of his wife, he couldn't accept the reality of her being gone. Lauren's presence was in every corner of the house they shared for 16 years. He heard her voice responding to his thoughts and when he said something humorous aloud, her laughter seeming audible and real.

Bryce had been assured by his therapist this was not unusual, he wasn't going crazy or on the verge of a nervous breakdown. People work through their grief in different ways, he was told. Bryce tried to immerse himself in work, but since he and Lauren had been partners in their successful San Francisco law firm, Gibson & Gibson, her memory was omnipresent in his work too.

They met in law school at the University of Oregon. Lauren was from Sacramento, Bryce from Seattle. They fell in love before the end of the first term and were convinced, in a jovial way, that because it was providential for them to have met half way geographically, it was an imperative to always meet half way in all aspects of their life together. They married in the summer and lived on student loans and part-time jobs until they finished their degrees.

It was a good match, but not without struggles and rough patches to work on and through. Bryce was quiet, thoughtful and considered by some to be reserved. Lauren was sparkling, vivacious, athletic and full of good humor. Bryce specialized in civil and corporate law; Lauren began her career as a public defender before becoming a much-sought-after criminal lawyer.

Although they desperately wanted to have children, that was not to be. After Lauren's second difficult miscarriage they agreed with her doctor to have a tubal ligation. Bryce – in a show of loving support – had a vasectomy the following week, telling Lauren after the fact. She was not pleased.

"What if something happens to me?" she demanded to know, "and you have a chance for children with someone else."

"First of all," Bryce answered calmly, "nothing is going to happen to you – you won't let it; and secondly, if we can't have our children, I wouldn't be interested in having any with someone else."

Sixteen years later Lauren would be dead. She suffered massive trauma by slamming into a large tree in an attempt to avoid a crash with a maverick skier while challenging a dangerous ski run just outside the Seefeld Resort near Mittenwald, Germany. The skier causing the accident was never identified.

In addition to her deep and abiding love for Bryce, Lauren had two burning passions – her work as a lawyer and skiing. Her father, Bill Fiedler, an Olympic slalom racer who came within two seconds of claiming the bronze medal in 1960 at Squaw Valley, had Lauren on the slopes as soon as she could walk. He would alternate their weekend outings between Squaw Valley and Sierra Summit Mountain. By age five she was skiing challenging slopes with amazing ease and agility.

Her father had encouraged Lauren to follow his example and train for the Olympics, but her life was filled with too many interests and diverse activities to concentrate on a single goal. However, skiing for recreation and sheer enjoyment remained at the top of her list.

Good skiing was readily available within a four-hour driving distance of their home in Sausalito, and they spent as many weekends as their schedules allowed heading for the mountains. Lauren would ski; Bryce would lug along his laptop and briefcase stuffed with office work. A month each spring or fall would find them traveling somewhere in Europe. These junkets were done with the understanding that one day, two full winter months would be devoted to alpine skiing for Lauren. Bryce would take short day trips by train to explore local villages. She and Bryce agreed to combine their love of travel with visiting ski resorts whenever possible and, prior to the time of her accident, had enjoyed most of the ski areas in the west.

While in fourth grade, Bryce became enamored with history and he followed that interest through college, graduating with a degree in European history as well as political science. He surrounded himself with history books. A picture in his middle school geography book of the Danube flowing through Budapest was indelibly etched on his brain. For years he dreamed of the possibility of visiting as much of the continent as possible while he and Lauren were young and healthy enough to get the full benefit of the experiences.

Their European visits, over a span of nine years included – in the aggregate – England, Ireland, Belgium, The Netherlands, Germany, the Czech Republic, Hungary (where they fell in love with Budapest), Austria, Switzerland, Italy, Spain and France. Arriving home after their last trip, which concluded with two full weeks in Paris, Lauren announced with gleeful, savored vengeance it was now time to "hit the Alps."

The two-month excursion beginning in Mittenwald was to be the first stop of four in the Alps. Another "meeting-half-way" example of compromise. From Seefeld they would follow the Olympic route Lauren's father had taken as a contestant – Innsbruck, Austria to Grenoble, France and finally to Sarajevo, where he served as a coach to the U.S. team during the 1984 games.

Left-brained Bryce loved all the planning that came with travel. Before each trip he would surround himself with maps, airline schedules, Eurail timetables and hotel websites. In preparing for Lauren's "great skiing extravaganza" as he called it, he gave special attention to working out the smallest details. This was her trip. She would be the snow queen of Europe and he would revel in his role as travel agent, transportation facilitator, house boy, masseur and photographer.

This was truly the quid pro quo of love and life. While Bryce didn't embrace religion, seldom did a night pass without his giving thanks to someone bigger and smarter, than he for his good fortune.

The flight attendant's welcoming announcement through the public address system snapped Bryce out of his pensiveness and he watched through the window as the Boeing 777 pushed back from the gate. He became aware of someone being seated next to him. One of the luxuries in which he and Lauren indulged was flying first-class. Though luxury wasn't high on their list of priorities, and though they preferred two-star hotels and small B & B's for their overnights, arriving at their destination rested and well-fed was worth the extra air fare.

Glancing up, Bryce – who had hoped for an unoccupied seat next to his – was disconcerted to realize a woman would be seated there for the duration of the flight. Was relieved somewhat, however, when he saw she was wearing a wedding ring.

Taking some time to get herself and her belongings settled, she apologized by saying "Sorry about all the fuss. You can probably tell I'm not an experienced overseas traveler."

Bryce didn't respond, returning his attention to the window. A light rain was falling; thunderstorms were predicted.

As the plane reached the taxiing apron and began its slow crawl awaiting takeoff instructions, Bryce was again annoyed by the woman unzipping her carryon bag, rummaging through its contents and rezipping the bag before sliding it under the seat in front of her. She then appeared to become very tense, breathing heavily.

Bryce was about to ask her if she was feeling okay but kept quiet when he saw her eyes were tightly closed and she was clutching a rosary. Her fingers moved from bead to bead rapidly, her lips moving. Bryce was, at the same time, intrigued with and concerned about her behavior so he continued to watch her closely.

Her intense rosary activity quieted some as the plane ascended and when the copilot informed the passengers the cruising altitude had been reached. She exhaled audibly, opened her eyes and let the rosary fall into her lap.

Aware that Bryce was watching her with some concern, she smiled and said with a tone of quasi-sincerity, "Well, I got us off the ground safely; let's hope I do as well when we land."

Bryce smiled. "If that's what it takes, you go for it." He added, "Is that string of beads your lucky charm?"

"Well, sort of I guess. It's something I do every day as part of my routine; I just go at it harder and faster when I'm on an airplane. I haven't flown much but each time I do, I make sure Heaven knows I'm on board. So far, so good."

"Where are you headed?" Bryce asked, trying to be courteous, momentarily forgetting it was a direct flight to London's Heathrow airport.

"You mean, from London?" she replied.

"Yeah, right. Are you staying around Jolly Old London, or just passing through?"

"I'm going to Ireland to visit my brother and a part of our family I haven't seen since I was 12. My aunt and uncle are getting along in years and I've a couple of cousins I'd like to get better acquainted with. My brother is a priest who has dual citizenship. He splits his parish assignments between Ireland and the U.S.

He's in Ireland for another three years. They all live in a small town about an hour west of Dublin."

"So, were you born in Ireland?"

"No, just my father. He immigrated to the U.S. with his parents when he was young. Granddad moved to Philadelphia to spread the word for that wondrous Irish elixir, Guinness beer. My father worked for Granddad and took over the business when Granddad retired and moved back to Ireland. Later, when Granddad passed, we went to Galway for his wake, which lasted four days. That's the only time I've been outside the U.S."

Her gleaming smile was disarming. Even if she hadn't mentioned her Irish heritage, it would have been obvious to Bryce. Her shoulder-length dark red hair and dancing emerald eyes were clear giveaways. From his memory of old Turner Classic Movies, Bryce conjured up Maureen O'Hara sitting in the seat next to him.

"And how about you?" she asked. "Is London your final destination?"

"No, it's only the beginning. I'll be in Europe for sometime – undetermined, as yet."

Bryce realized immediately he had said too much to this total stranger; a clear case of talking before thinking. He excused himself and went to the lavatory. After splashing water on his face and drying his hands, he stood looking into the mirror. The man he saw reflected was nothing like the one he remembered, but fit the way he felt: tired, old, listless, confused and lonely. Oh, he was so lonely. And oh, how he missed Lauren. All the emotion of missing her was intensified by the realization he was on his way to revisit so many places they'd been together. If he were somewhere other than here in this lavatory on this plane, tears would be flowing. But this wasn't the place or time for tears.

Regaining his composure, he returned to his seat, the woman smiled a brief acknowledgment before continuing to read Vogue magazine. Bryce stared out the window at the dark clouds hanging below, watching the bursts of lightening like so many fireworks. He was thankful to be flying well above the outside turbulence; the storm raging inside his body was more than enough to cope with.

The flight attendant came by taking beverage orders and handing out dinner menus. It was only then Bryce turned away from the window.

"Can I buy you a drink?" he asked his seat mate. This was a rhetorical question since he knew and she knew the drinks were free; but it sounded better to him than "would you join me for a drink." He fought back the tear that might have come when he realized what he had asked the woman was his standard question to Lauren.

"A glass of red wine would be good before dinner," she answered. "It's been a rather long day and the night will be even longer. I can't sleep on a plane."

The two didn't speak again until the flight attendant returned carrying a bottle of Merlot, two crystal wine glasses and a basket containing a corkscrew, a variety of gourmet crackers with small squares of brie and Gouda cheese.

"Should I open the bottle or would you like to do the honors?" the attendant asked Bryce.

"That's something I can handle," Bryce replied, reaching for the corkscrew.

When the glasses were appropriately half-filled, the bouquet sniffed, and the wine swirled to test its legs, Bryce announced, "This seems to be a very fine vintage, tart but not sassy; bold without being pretentious."

They both laughed.

"I have no idea what I just said," Bryce admitted.

"Nor do I," she smiled. "But it sounded good. Shall we propose a toast?"

"That would be nice. You go first."

"OK, here's a good old fashioned Irish friendship toast." They raised their glasses.

"May there always be work for your hands to do; may your purse always hold a coin or two; may the sun always shine on your windowpane; may a rainbow be certain to follow each rain; may the hand of a friend always be near you; may God fill your heart with gladness to cheer you; and may you be in Heaven a half hour before the devil knows you're dead."

She offered the poem in a slow, deliberate cadence, letting each thought sink in before going to the next. Their eyes met as the two glasses clinked. They took a slow sip, and smiled.

"Now it's your turn."

Bryce thought solemnly for a moment before raising his glass and speaking.

"May my sentimental journey be what it needs to be."

Her questioning look was obvious as they touched glasses and sipped.

"Do you care to tell me what that means? It sounds very personal, but I did drink to it. Is it something you can – or even want to share?"

"I'm not sure I can." Bryce hesitated for a long moment before adding, "But maybe I need to. You're very easy to talk with."

"I'm a good listener, and we have a lot of time to kill before we get to London." She flashed a quick smile. "Just say what you want, or can, or need to. In a few hours we'll part company, so your secrets will be safe with me." Again that smile.

"No secrets, I assure you. Just thoughts and feelings. But before I get started, could I ask you a personal question?"

"Sure, I guess. If it's too personal, I'll let you know."

"Okay, here goes. Would you tell me your name?"

The question caught her in the middle of a wine sip and she fought hard to swallow it before bursting into laughter. Her laugh was full and rich and contagious. Bryce caught the bug. Other nearby passengers joined in and soon the cabin was filled with smiles and chuckles – laughing at nothing but the fun Bryce and the woman seemed to be having.

"Of course I'll tell you my name. But you have to get ready for it. There will be a test at the end, so pay close attention. I was christened Teresa Roisin Alana Caitlin Irene Dunne. It's an Irish thing. The first two names are for my grandmothers, the second two for my father's favorite aunts, and the last for my mother's favorite movie actress. My mother and my teachers called me Teresa, my father called me Teresa Roisin unless he was angry with me; then I'd get the full slate, including Dunne. My brother chose to call me Cait, as did many of my friends. One day in grade nine I was doodling with all five given names and realized by taking the first letter of each I could be called Traci.

"Traci caught on quickly with all my friends, but was never acknowledged by either my parents or my teachers. My brother stuck with Cait. So there you have it. Any questions?"

"No questions. And I can't pass the test."

"So, what about you? What's your name?"

"Nothing so complicated. I'm Bryce Gibson. My mother chose Bryce because all the good names for children of hippies had been taken. You know, like Birchbark and Starfish and Cloudburst. So I got stuck with an almost real-person name."

"No middle name?"

"Yes, but I don't use it. For official signing purposes, I use an initial."

"And the initial is . . . ?"

Bryce hesitated before saying softly, "C."

"No, no, no!" Traci blurted, gleefully. "Your name is Bryce Canyon Gibson! I love it!"

Dinner was being served. Traci selected chicken cordon bleu as her entrée and Bryce chose peppered swordfish steak. Each came with a small Caesar salad, new potatoes, and asparagus al dente. Bryce requested the red Merlot wine be replaced with a white Riesling. Dessert, with coffee and brandy, would come later.

Conversation between the two was reduced to comments regarding the meal and the lack of turbulence thus far on the flight. When dessert was offered, both selected warm apple strudel with a topping of French vanilla ice cream. Traci thought hot tea would be nice; Bryce opted for black coffee. Both passed on the brandy.

After the dinner trays were taken away and beverage cups refilled, Traci reached for the in-flight entertainment guide and began reading the card.

"I'm sorry, Traci," Bryce said. "I'm not ignoring you or forgetting that you're curious about the meaning of my toast. It's a hard thing for me to think about, and I've never talked to anyone – except my shrink – about it, though he's encouraged me talk and share with others."

"It's okay, Bryce. You're right, I am curious about what sort of sentimental journey you're on, and why you're taking it. But talk about it only if you're comfortable. I'm enjoying your company; I don't want to put a damper on our conversation." Looking back at the flight entertainment guide, Traci added, "There are a couple of good movies listed here we could watch."

"Thanks for giving me an out. It's difficult to know where to begin, but I would like to talk. It's been a couple of months since I got teary in my therapy session, so I'm doing better."

Traci squeezed Bryce's arm for a few seconds. "One of my favorite authors C. S. Lewis, in his book The Silver Chair said something that has been very helpful to me. 'Crying is all right as long as it lasts, but sooner or later you have to decide what to do'."

Bryce sighed deeply as he reached for the half-empty wine bottle. Moving the bottle toward Traci's glass, she put her hand over the rim, signaling she was good. Bryce poured his glass full and took a large swallow.

Bryce began in slow, measured sentences, telling Traci of Lauren, how they met and fell in love, how their marriage was blessed by family and friends, how their up-front agreement to always be willing to compromise when they differed had made their bond grow stronger as the years went by, how they leaned on each other in developing their successful careers. Finally he told Traci of Lauren's death 16 months before.

He spoke of Lauren's beauty, charm and outgoing personality being the perfect foil to his quiet, studious demeanor. The more he talked the more it seemed to Traci he was becoming less uptight. He began punctuating the historical narrative with anecdotes, sometimes inserted with a chuckle or a shake of the head. He boasted of Lauren's talent in the courtroom, her skiing ability, and their shared love of traveling.

"I try to work through all the 'what-ifs'. I know nothing can change. I know nothing will bring Lauren back, but my brain doesn't want to cooperate with reality. So it keeps asking, 'What if Lauren was a less adventurous skier? What if we had gone to Sarajevo first instead of Seefeld? What if the other skier hadn't forced her off the trail into the trees? What if . . . what if. . . . I have to get off the 'what-if' spinning wheel."

Bryce paused for some time, considering how much more to share, then poured the last of the wine into his glass, and continued.

"The last, and most lasting, memory I have of our being in Europe was those final, terrible days after her accident when she was broken and battered, paralyzed from her neck down. I was at her bedside from the minute I reached the hospital until the minute she died.

"Only once did she open her eyes. She recognized me and tried to smile. I kissed her and told her how much I loved her and I was going to make sure she pulled through. Her last, barely audible words were, 'please don't; if you love me, please let me go'. Her body was too broken to keep going."

Bryce stared straight ahead, getting a grip on his inner turmoil.

"I signed some forms. The next morning doctors removed her from the resuscitation machine. In less than an hour this beautiful, smart, energetic, athletic and – most of all – loving part of my life was gone.

"At that moment, the mother of all 'what-ifs' hit me full force. What if a miracle would have happened, making her totally well again and I had taken that chance away by letting her die?"

They sat quietly for a few minutes, Bryce looking out the window, Traci looking at Bryce. Then she spoke.

"Bryce, you need to know a miracle did happen. It was the miracle the two of you shared for 20 years. The miracle of meeting and falling in love; of building a future together; of seeing love grow deeper every day, during good times and bad; of having an understanding that your differences could be resolved by talking them through and compromising. This miracle isn't a 'what-if', it's a 'what-was'.

"Oh, sure, this isn't as dramatic or obvious as a blind person regaining sight or a deaf person being able to hear; or a quadriplegic suddenly jumping up and running a four-minute mile. But, believe me, in today's world, the life you describe with Lauren was totally miraculous."

The cabin lights had been turned off and the sky glowed in pastels of red and orange as the sun hung in space between dusk and dawn. Bryce turned his face toward the window and rubbed his eyes with the heel of his hand. He felt the gentle touch of Traci once again squeezing his arm and realized from the movement of the touch she cared about his pain.

Quickly, Bryce cleared his throat and continued.

"So here's the 'sentimental journey' part. It's my therapist's recommendation. No, it's more than a recommendation, it's an insistence. I have a hunch he's becoming weary or bored – or both – with my lack of progress getting on top of things. He's concerned I'm beginning to fixate on Lauren's death at the expense of her life, our life together, and certainly at the expense of getting on with my life; whatever this life holds.

"I have an open-return airline ticket valid for three months and a three-month Eurail pass. So. . . I'm returning to many places Lauren and I visited; places that sparked special feelings. Places where we had the most fun, and – as best I can – relive those times as a way to gain perspective on my life as it is now. She was an excellent writer and kept journals of all our trips.   When I get to a city, or village, or just swaying along on the train, I'll read her thoughts and impressions and remember those times through her words."

"I don't know who your therapist is," Traci said, "but he's worth every penny of his fee. Where will you be going?"

"I spent a lot of time trying to decide. I'm sort of a nerd when it comes to planning and record keeping. I've put together an itinerary which takes into account what I call a 'must go' factor. We visited so many places, trying to hit them all again would be impossible. So I reviewed our trip data, operating on the premise that the more times we returned to a place, the more we must have enjoyed it.

"So, with this less-than-scientific approach, the two top 'must-goes' turned out to be London and Paris. The other spots making the list are Provence and Metz in France; Bruges in Belgium; Budapest; Salzburg in Austria; Prague; Barcelona, Florence, Italy; and the Basque Country on the Atlantic coast. So I'll start in London, make a big clockwise sweep around the continent and end in Paris. The projected route is London, Bruges, Metz, Prague, Budapest, Salzburg, Florence, Arles, Barcelona, Basque Country and Paris."

"Wow, that's really impressive," Traci said in all sincerity. "May I ask a question?"

"Of course you may."

"You don't have Ireland on your list. Have you never been there or didn't it meet your criteria for a return visit?"

"The answer is 'yes' and 'yes'. Yes, we were there for a week or so some years back as an 'add-on' trip. We found ourselves in the Normandy region of France and realized we were near the town of Roscoff, a cross-channel port for the Irish Ferry Line. We decided on a whim to ferry across to Rosslare and take the train on to Dublin. The crossing took 17 hours, but the ferry was complete with restaurants, pubs with entertainment, gambling casinos, pool halls, clothing shops and beauty parlor.

"Presumably, because we'd not done our homework, we weren't prepared to fit this larger-than-expected city into our time limits. So our Dublin experience was an evening walkabout with one night in a hotel before hopping on a train heading west for Limerick. Lauren was very good about arranging for lodging through local tourist information offices, opting whenever possible to fine quaint inns or B & B's. After hearing what we would like, the woman at the Limerick tourist office recommended a four-room B & B in the village of Adare, a half-hour bus ride away, and phoned for our reservation.

"That B & B was our base for immersing ourselves in the pulse of life in Ireland as best we could in a week's time. We became regulars at one of the two of Adare's pubs, took long walks each morning in the village and surrounding countryside and thoroughly enjoyed the experience.

"It was a pleasant experience and one I might repeat someday. I'd like to give Dublin a better chance too. I just couldn't fit it into this trip."

"Do you have reservations in all the towns you'll be visiting?"

"Only in London and Paris – at places we always stayed. Having specific arrival and departure dates lock you into a schedule and doesn't allow for much spontaneity. The beauty of a Eurail pass is you can be amazingly flexible; and the rail systems in Europe are outstanding. For us, accommodations were secondary considerations so long as they were convenient, clean and secure. And for Lauren, touches of authentic local décor lent value-added charm."

Traci was quiet for some time, trying to absorb the bits and pieces of Bryce's collage of memories of his life with Lauren, how they fit; how lonely he must be. Some tragedies were never to be understood.

She interrupted her thoughts.

"Do you keep in touch with your office?"

"I do – with an extremely good staff. My three junior partners can handle anything that comes their way and I have an administrative assistant with an iron fist covered by a velvet glove. I've set a phone schedule with her. A couple times a week when I can, I'll check email."

Contrary to her earlier statement that she couldn't relax on a plane, when Bryce returned to his seat from a trip to the lavatory, he found Traci wrapped in a blanket, sleeping peacefully. He was relieved not to try and make more small talk. He reached for a pillow and placed it behind his head. Before he had any chance to review the events of this most unusual day, his screen went blank.

CHAPTER TWO

"GOOD morning ladies and gentlemen. This is your captain. We are approximately two hours and 15 minutes from touchdown at Heathrow International, arriving at Terminal Four. We have clear weather and visibility is ten miles. On our final approach, those of you on the right side of the aircraft should get a good look at Windsor Castle. In a few minutes the flight attendants will be serving breakfast. They will also distribute landing cards which must be completed and turned in to immigration officials at the passport checkpoint inside the terminal. Now sit back and enjoy the rest of our flight; and thank you for flying the Friendly Skies."

The announcement jolted Traci from her slumber. She woke with a start and reflectively and made quiet, wake up sounds. She looked around quickly to assess the extent of her pudency and found Bryce smiling at her.

"Good morning, Ms. Van Winkle."

"Oh, my word," Traci responded. "I guess that's why I've never let myself sleep on a plane. The waking up part is pretty embarrassing."

"My problem is snoring when I'm airborne," Bryce confessed. "I don't know why, I never snore anywhere else. At the end of a long flight I could guess how noisy I'd been by the number of bruises Lauren had inflicted on my ribcage."

"My father was a world-class snorer," Traci chuckled. "Sitting up, laying down, leaning against a wall – anywhere. My mother slept with him for fifty-three years, wearing ear plugs. The night of the day he died," Traci's voice softened and took on a solemn tone, "I heard my mother crying in their room. When I went to comfort her, I saw she had buttoned his pajama top around a large pillow and was holding it tightly in her arms. In her firm but loving voice she was pleading 'snore, darn you, snore'."

As Traci went to the lavatory to freshen up before breakfast was served, Bryce reflected on the kind of relationship Traci's parents must have shared compared to that of his own parents. Bryce's father, Andrew Craig – a self-styled anti-Viet Nam hippie who chose to go by the name Free Bird – fled to Canada to avoid the military draft, leaving Bryce's mother to fend for herself while raising an infant son. Having a dependent child allowed Free Bird to apply for a deferment from the draft; but he considered that route "cowardly." He had led demonstrations, encouraging other young men to join him in burning their selective service cards. Fleeing the country was the ultimate protest.

Bryce's mother, Elaine Roberts – a.k.a. Spring Breeze – was a self employed house cleaner during the day and tended bar three nights a week. While his mother worked, Bryce was cared for, on no particular rotating schedule, by his two grandmothers and a spinster aunt. Free Bird left for Canada with the promise he would return when the war ended. He kept in touch for the first six months with letters postmarked from towns in British Columbia and the Yukon Territory; but then the letters stopped.

The two hadn't married. That would have meant recognizing the establishment. Spring Breeze tried her best to provide a good home for Bryce but after three years of struggling to get by, she turned him over to the Washington Department of Health and Social Services for placement in foster care or adoption. After only a few months of living with foster parents, Bryce was legally adopted by a childless couple – the father a successful business man, the mother a former debutante – who fell in love with Bryce the minute they saw him.

The couple, Gregory and Melissa Gibson, encouraged Bryce's biological mother, once again using her real name, Elaine, to stay in contact with Bryce. They kept his first and middle given names out of consideration to Elaine.

When Bryce was five, Elaine took him on an outing to the zoo and told him she was getting married and she and her husband would be moving to Ohio. The wedding ceremony was simple but classy, held in the backyard of the Gibson's home. Five-year-old Bryce gave his mother away after walking her down a path strewn with rose petals. There was a small reception; Elaine gave Bryce a hug and kisses and drove away with her new husband, marking the last time Bryce was with Elaine.

"I hope I repaired some of the damage," Traci said with a smile as she slid gracefully into her seat.

She had made good use of her time. Her makeup was perfect

and she was wearing a hint of a subtle but distinctive perfume, reminding Bryce just how very selective and particular Lauren was in her choice of perfumes. During their first trip to Paris she had spent the better part of a week on the Right Bank visiting parfum boutiques on Faubourg, St. Honore, Avenue Montaigne, the Champs-Elysees and Place Vendome.

Her final choice was expensive, but definitely her. She used it often, but sparingly, and always managed to return to Paris before her supply ran out.

"While you were in the repair shop," Bryce quipped, "I was thinking about your parents and wondering how much influence they've had on your life."

"If we had a year or so to discuss it, I suppose I could cover the subject. They were wonderful parents. No, they were wonderful people who were also my parents. My mother was a true saint. She understood everyone's needs and tried to meet them without being condescending. She was gentle but firm in her child-rearing style. She could discipline with a stare, a hug, and a smile.

"My father, by contrast, met everything head on. He was a big man with a big heart and – some would say – a big mouth. He loved being the Guinness distributor for the greater Philadelphia region. He was very gregarious and generous to a fault. For a few hours after work he could be found in one of his favorite Irish pubs like the Dark Horse, Northwest and North, Kildare's and Brittingham's. Not only was Guinness the drink of choice in these pubs, but a lot of food recipes included Guinness as an ingredient.

"He would lead the patrons in singing; beat everyone playing darts; and loved to take every opportunity to mix religion with politics. He took pride in bragging he was 'more Catholic than the Pope' and 'more Irish than St. Patrick'."

"Sounds like a great guy to me," Bryce said, smiling and slightly shaking his head. "Do you have a lot of siblings?"

"No, just my brother Michael. He's the only one."

"That surprises me. My understanding has always been Catholic families have more kids than most; and the same for the Irish."

"You're right on both counts," Traci laughed, "but less than a year after I was born, my father contracted a bad case of the mumps, resulting in becoming sterile. He was angry with God at first, but got over it. As a result, Michael and I got more of his attention than we would have otherwise."

"What about you?" Bryce asked. "Do you have a lot of kids?"

"I sure do," Traci replied, flashing a smile. "At last count I had 26."

Bryce's stunned expression made Traci quickly offer an explanation. "I'm a school teacher; I teach second grade."

"Whew! You don't have any children of your own?"

"No."

Bryce decided this was not a subject Traci wanted to continue, so after a moment he asked, "Do you have much of a layover before your flight to Dublin?"

"If everything's on schedule I shouldn't have more than a couple of hours."

They busied themselves filling out the required landing card information and finished just before the announcement was made they were descending for their landing into Heathrow.

"Excuse me," Traci said, reaching for the bag containing the rosary. "I'll see you when we've landed."

Inside the terminal, Bryce volunteered to walk Traci through the procedures, locating the checked luggage, clearing customs and immigration and finding which terminal housed Aer Lingus, the Irish airline that would take her to Dublin. Their arrival on United was directed to Terminal four; Traci's departure on Aer Lingus was from Terminal one.

"Come on," Bryce said as the two pulled their rolling luggage through the automatic doors separating the customs area from the arrival lounge. "Let's take a little train ride."

As they schlepped along, heading for the shuttle, Bryce explained that Heathrow consists of five separate terminals, each operating independently from the others. A very efficient rail system connects the terminals as well as linking with a London Underground train running on a timely schedule, carrying passengers into the city.

"London's big," Bryce continued, "but the transportation system is very easy once you get the hang of it."

After locating the Aer Lingus check-in counter and getting her boarding pass, the two found their way to a coffee bar and ordered lattes to help kill the hour before Traci's flight would leave. As they sipped their coffees, Bryce began singing the praises of London – its history, its museums, its monuments – until Traci asked through her flashing smile, "Are you sure you're not a lobbyist for the London Tourist Bureau?"

"I promise I'm not," Bryce chuckled. "But I love the history of centuries packed into this city. Other than Paris, Lauren and I spent more time here than anywhere else in Europe. You should give it a try sometime."

"With your enthusiasm for the place, I just might do that. In fact, I might possibly stop off for a few days on my return from visiting Michael. I'm planning to spend three weeks with him, but I could cut that a few days short. Do you have a hotel to recommend?"

"Most definitely. Remember, we like small, non-touristy places. With that in mind, you can't go wrong with the Edward Lear Hotel. It's a place without many amenities, but meets the criteria of small, clean and convenient. The people who run it are gracious and the breakfasts are hearty traditional English and give a good send off for the day. Lear, the 19th century artist and poet, lived in the house for a time."

"My goodness! I'm quite familiar with Lear," Traci said. "I even teach a unit on nonsense poems to my class, including some of Lear's poems. One of their favorites is The Owl and the Pussycat Went to Sea in a Beautiful Pea Green Boat. Do you have the address of the hotel?"

Bryce opened his briefcase and pulled out his printed itinerary and a business card. "Here's my card; I'll write the hotel's contact information on the back and let them know they might hear from you."

When it was time for Traci to enter the security area on her way to the departure gate, she took Bryce's hands tightly in hers.

"Thanks for an interesting time. It was a good flight and went quickly, thanks to you. I enjoyed getting acquainted. Lauren was a lucky girl. Enjoy the rest of your journey, Bryce Canyon Gibson."

"And you have a great time with your brother."

"I hope it will be. Michael has always been my very best friend – and confidant."

There she paused, during which she decided to share a glimpse into her otherwise undisclosed life.

"I'm going through a pretty rough time at the moment," she confided. "I'm counting on Michael's advice and counsel to help me smooth it out."

Bryce wondered if he'd missed something in their earlier conversation, but simply offered reassuringly, "I know whatever it is, he'll be a great help. Take care, Teresa Roisin Alana Caitlin Irene Dunne."

"Hey, you just passed the test. I'll put a gold star by your name."

Their eyes met briefly. Traci turned and walked quickly through the doorway leading to the security area, without looking back.

Pulling his roller bag toward the Heathrow Terminal One tube station, a sudden feeling of loneliness gripped Bryce. Was it because he was missing Lauren so terribly? Or was it from watching Traci walk away? There was something special, something comforting about Traci, a connection he had missed since Lauren's death. His twelve hours with Traci seemed much longer. The way in which she allowed, even quietly encouraged, him to open up and express his feelings provided a catharsis he desperately needed.

Then the feeling of loneliness gave way to one of disappointment. All he knew about Traci was her name and that she was a married school teacher. He hadn't asked enough questions. Where does she live? She talked about Philadelphia but boarded the plane in San Francisco. What is her married name? Did she keep 'Dunne' or did she take her husband's name; or is it one of those hyphenated melds? What is the rough time she's going through? Must be something serious if she was traveling to Ireland for Michael's advice.

By the time he reached the train platform, ticket in hand, he decided it was probably best he didn't have the answers. Getting to the Edward Lear and catching a power nap would put his journey back in perspective.

Bryce was pleased he remembered the tube route from Heathrow to the hotel without referring to a map. The Piccadilly line running from the airport to Cockfosters station in the north of London is the major link. Bryce knew to transfer from the Piccadilly to the District line at Earl's Court station then transfer at Notting Hill Gate station to the Central line. The third stop on the Central line is Marble Arch station, Bryce's stop.

As if he needed any reminder as to where in the world he might be, the recorded message of "Mind the Gap" each time the train doors opened was a reinforcement that he was back in London.

It was a short two-block walk from the underground station on Oxford Street north to Seymour Street where the hotel is located.

It was like returning home when he turned the corner and saw the sign for the hotel. He was sure he had noticed it before, but this time it took on new meaning. On the Edward Lear Hotel sign above the entry door was a hand painted picture of an owl and a pussy cat sitting in a pea green boat and hung as usual among baskets overflowing with flowers in season.

The desk clerk greeted Bryce warmly and expressed his condolences regarding Lauren's death. "We didn't want to believe the message you sent with your reservation request telling us of her accident. She was one of our very favorite people."

"Thank you. She always enjoyed staying here."

Their last visit to London had been quite a week – filled with extraordinary events. The day after their arrival, Prince Rainier of Monaco died. Two days later Pope John Paul's funeral was held in Rome. Prince Charles and Camilla Parker Bowles were married in St. George's Chapel at Windsor; Tony Blair began his reelection campaign.

————————

In his room, Bryce tried to take the nap he felt he needed, but had no luck. Lauren would have vetoed even the mention of napping. Her theory when arriving from an overseas flight was to go, go, go during daylight and hit the sack at a regular nighttime hour, bypassing jet lag. After a half hour of tossing, Bryce concluded her theory was right. He decided to take a walk; a route he and Lauren had traversed many times.

Just south of the Marble Arch is the northeast entrance to Hyde Park. This wasn't only an entrance to the park, but an entrance to memories of what they'd experienced and loved about London. The sprawl of the park in the heart of the sprawling city; clearly England with Bobbies in evidence; the traditional striped white and green lawn chairs scattered about the expanse of lawns. They enjoyed strolling along, holding hands and laughing; stopping on Sundays at Speaker's Corner to listen to overlapping and competitive oration; watching the interested and disinterested folks standing or milling about. Only in London!

At Serpentine Lake they would decide whether to go west and visit the beauty of Kensington Gardens or east and on to Buckingham Palace. On this balmy afternoon, Bryce chose to head east, go through the gate at Hyde Park Corner and stop to rest on the steps of Wellington's Monument.

He and Lauren enjoyed Buckingham and the pomp associated with it, especially if they happened to be around at the Changing of the Guard; but the crowds were usually so large that finding a viewing place was difficult. So they walked on to either Green Park or St. James Park, those elegant spaces, sometimes taking time to sit on a park bench, still caught up in the experience so uniquely British.

On their last visit to London with the masses they watched the Changing of the Guard – complete with the Royal Marching Band. Then as they walked down the Mall toward Clarence House, with its posted Royal Guard, they were passed by the "on foot" regiment on their way back toward their barracks near Whitehall. Lauren noted in her journal, "*All very serendipitous, an exquisite memory.*"

Bryce was creating today's walking tour as he went along. From the Palace he headed south on Buckingham Road, spent a few minutes in the Queen's Gallery gift shop, looked into the Royal Mews, and ended up inside Victoria Station. Once there, and needing 25 pence to get into the men's room, he realized he didn't have any British pounds. He had used his credit card for the two purchases he had made: the lattes at Heathrow and the train ticket into London.

He knew where to find an ATM and withdrew £250. His itinerary for London had been set in a random list. He knew places he wanted to revisit, but hadn't worked out the logistics. There were three day trips on the list: Windsor Castle, Bath Spa and Oxford. Before leaving Victoria Station he picked up a train schedule for Bath Spa, which departs from Paddington Station, then crossed Elizabeth Street to the Green Line bus station for a schedule to Windsor. On his way west to Ebury Street he ducked into the Victoria Coach Station and got the bus schedule to Oxford.

During their first few trips to London, he and Lauren had stayed at a small B & B on Ebury Street located in the Belgravia district. In preparing for another visit, Bryce was told the inn would be closed for renovations. A friend of Lauren's recommended the Edward Lear as an alternative, and the rest was history.

They did return to Ebury Street on several London visits, to eat at The Plumber's Pub, a neighborhood pub they'd enjoyed when staying nearby. It lacked the boisterousness of Irish pubs, but had excellent food. Bryce, realizing he hadn't eaten since the light breakfast on the plane, reasoned a hearty meal at The Plumber's Pub would tide him over until breakfast.

CHAPTER THREE

AFTER enjoying a hearty meal of fish and chips during last afternoon's visit to The Plumber's Pub, Bryce had gone back to Victoria Station to buy a Three Day Travel Card, good for both the bus line and underground. The lawyer in Bryce compelled him to read most small-print conditions even on such things as travel passes, so when he noticed his card was 'Issued Subject to Conditions – See Over', he couldn't resist. The "Conditions of Carriage" were pretty standard and straightforward; but the final warning, set apart from the Conditions paragraph, was curious at best.

"Purchasing tickets from a ticket tout could result in the buyer being prosecuted."

There was no threat to the seller, only to the buyer. Lauren would have loved it. "How very British," Bryce could hear her saying.

With pass in hand, Bryce boarded a Victoria Line train and rode north one stop to the Green Park station then transferred to the Jubilee Line for a one-stop jaunt to Bond Street station. From there he decided to walk along Oxford Street back to the hotel as he and Lauren had done so many times.

He walked slowly, taking in the sights and sounds that stirred his memory of Lauren's interest and exuberance for all things British. How he missed her. He stopped to read the poster advertising the current offerings at the multiplex cinema where they had been patrons. The last movie they attended there was Miss Congeniality.

The Marks & Spencer store on Oxford was still open, a handy location for everything from packaged salads to take to your room, good wine, replenishing sundries or finding a good book. Before leaving the store Bryce bought a package of chocolate mint cookies, Lauren's favorite.

Later that evening in bed, Bryce fell asleep studying travel schedules.

————————

The travel clock alarm went off at 6:30, rousing Bryce from a deep sleep. Lauren had named the little clock 'cricket' because of its chirping sound. As usual, Bryce had placed 'cricket' across the room so he couldn't reach out and put the clock into snooze mode. Not ready for the day, but needing to put an end to the annoying chirp, Bryce rolled out of bed and turned off the alarm.

The aroma of brewing coffee drifting from the breakfast room was the final stimulus Bryce needed to shave, shower, get dressed for the day and go downstairs. When he entered the room, it was just as he remembered. The same tables with plastic flowers in plastic vases, the same chairs, the same cereal bar with choices of mixed-grain, corn flakes, or Rice Crispies. The beverage bar still held coffee in carafes, hot water for cocoa, cold milk for cereal, warm milk for coffee, apple juice, orange juice and prune juice. Tea drinkers were served at the table to assure steaming hot tea. Bananas and apples were in a bowl for the taking.

Bryce poured a cup of coffee, setting the cup on a table to claim his space and returned for juice. Once seated, a young woman with a pleasant smile brought him a rack of toast.

"What'll it be today, luv?" she asked. "The full Monty?"

"Yes, please, that would be great. Eggs scrambled."

Bryce was amused at the question, although he had heard it before. The "full Monty" is B & B lingo for the traditional English breakfast: Eggs, ham or bacon, stewed tomatoes, and what would pass in the States as pork 'n beans straight from a can, warmed a bit. In some cases blood sausage (a.k.a. blood pudding) when available, may be substituted for the bacon or ham. Lauren was fond of blood sausage.

As Bryce's breakfast was being served with the warning "be careful, the plate is hot," a man wearing a tweed jacket with leather elbow patches, a polka dot ascot, and pencil-thin moustache made a hand motion asking if he might sit at the table. Although two tables were unoccupied, the man pulled out a chair and sat down before waiting for Bryce to acknowledge his request.

Bryce was delighted to hear the man introduce himself with a heavy Scottish brogue. They exchanged pleasantries for a half-hour, talking about the global economy ("It's the Chinese we really need to keep an eye on, ya know?"), the new British Prime Minister ("He's an old Scotsman, ya know?"), whether the Queen will ever step down and let Charles have his turn ("She really doesn't like Camilla much, ya know?").

Before their first trip to England, a colleague of Bryce and Lauren had observed, "Englishmen, on first meeting, seem to be very aloof and reserved. And they are – until you ask them a question – then seemingly endless conversation will follow."

Bryce excused himself saying he needed to get on with his busy day.

"An' what'll ya be doin', Laddie?"

"Taking a day trip to Bath Spa," Bryce answered, although he wasn't really sure what the day might shape up to be.

The two shook hands, wished each other well and Bryce headed quickly to his room. Recalling their friend's caution concerning asking a question of an Englishman, Bryce reflected, "Scotsmen don't even have to be asked."

While the breakfast response to the man's question was the first thing that came to mind, Bryce looked carefully at the train schedule from Paddington to Bath. He remembered it was an easy day trip with travel times no more than an hour and thirty minutes from station to station. Of the three short jaunts from London on his itinerary, Bath was the farthest out; so why not go there first?

The last time he and Lauren went to Bath for the day was to see about lodging for two nights when Bryce's parents would be with them. The Gibson's were seasoned travelers with numerous business trips, mostly to Hawaii, Hong Kong, Singapore and Malaysia. Bryce went with them to Hong Kong for two weeks during his junior year in high school, but had no desire to return to Asia.

Lauren wanted her in-laws to have the best possible time on this first trip to Europe. She had a special fondness for Bath, its Georgian architecture, its Cotswold's setting, and its historical span across centuries from the days of Roman occupation. So Lauren insisted their itinerary include a couple of days in Bath.

The city of Bath has a fascinating history. Some would say the most fascinating in all of England. Bath, along with Hadrian's Wall in the north of England, has the most outstanding and best preserved Roman remains in the country.

The city is aptly named as it originated and grew around its hot spring waters. Looking out across the city in any direction, the view is dominated by 17th century Georgian architecture, elegant and stately, all built from the soft, yellow Cotswold's sandstone. But here and there is a remarkable mix of Roman and medieval influence. Legend has it that Bladud, son of Hudibras, the eighth king of the Britons, founded the city in 863 BC. Some give credence to this belief due to the fact that two of the city's spas have statues of Bladud.

Bryce caught the nine thirty train to Bath from Paddington Station. Arriving early, he sat on a bench in front of the large statue of Paddington Bear and wandered through a souvenir shop. Lauren had started a Paddington collection of small stuffed bears and story books. He would purchase something to add to the collection when he returned from Bath.

Riding through the countryside listening to the clickety-clack of the train wheels on the rails, Bryce was reminded of the beauty of rural England. Lush green rolling hills provided a perfect panorama for reflection and soul searching. With each day he was becoming more convinced his therapist had written the right prescription. Reliving shared moments of happiness can be healing and happiness soon washes sadness away, renewing ones strength and purpose.

Reality was beginning to find its place in his mind and heart. Lauren is gone forever, but never forgotten; she made him strong by being strong. Now he needs to look deeply inside his soul to reassemble that strength, reestablish his priorities and get with the program.

It was a beautiful day in Bath. On his walk from the train station to the city's main square, Bryce passed by the hotel where they stayed – the Park Parade – and entered the lobby for a few minutes before going on.

Bryce checked the concert schedule for Bath Abbey and was glad to find there was an organ recital slated for three o'clock in the afternoon; his return train would leave at four thirty. It was a short walk from the Abbey to the station so he decided to stroll about, revisiting Putney Bridge, The Circus and the Royal Crescent. He wanted another look inside the Roman Baths, so before the concert he would have a late lunch in the Pump Room, the social heart of Bath for two centuries and still emitting an aura of social grace.

On his walk back to the train station he stopped at the Sally Lunn Bakery to pick up a box of Sally Lunn Buns for the Edward Lear Hotel staff. These buns have been made in this building according to a unique and secret recipe since the mid 1400's, for 600 years! Culinary and architectural histories meet!

––––––––––––––––

It was after seven when Bryce reached the hotel. The desk clerk was not on duty, but Bryce noticed a light coming from the small office at the end of the hallway and knocked on the door to deliver the buns.

"Oh, Mr. Gibson," the office employee said. "I'm so glad you're back. A woman phoned for you about an hour ago. I taped a message to your room door so you wouldn't miss it. Her name is Traci; she seemed quite anxious to speak with you. She'll be calling again at eight o'clock. I'll put her right through to your room. And thanks so much for the yummy buns."

Bryce sat on the edge of his bed staring blankly at the note. Questions ran through his head faster than he could hope to guess the answers. Traci had planned to stay in Ireland for three weeks. When they said goodbye at Heathrow, he supposed he would never see her again. He was now, at once, pleased and confused as to why she was trying to contact him. The little cricket clock on the dresser seemed to be standing still, as if trying to postpone reaching eight.

The loud ring of the phone made Bryce jump.

"Hello. This is Bryce Gibson."

"Bryce. This is Traci Dunne. Sorry to bother you but my visit with Michael didn't go well and I left. Since I have over two weeks before my flight home, I've decided to spend some time in London. I'm calling to see if you would still be there."

"Where are you now?"

"In a hotel at the Dublin airport. I have a flight out at ten o five in the morning."

"For Heathrow?"

"Yes. I spoke with the woman at your hotel just now and reserved a room for tomorrow night."

"What flight are you on? I'll meet your plane."

"Oh, Bryce, that's sweet of you but I don't want to disrupt your plans. I'll take a taxi; I'll be fine."

"My plans are made day-to-day. In the morning I plan to go to Heathrow and meet your plane."

After Traci reluctantly gave him the flight information and ended the call, Bryce prepared for bed and lay on his back staring at the ceiling until the activities of the day finally caught up with his mind and body and he fell asleep.

Rather than taking a chance of getting caught in a lengthy

breakfast discussion – always a possibility at the Edward Lear – Bryce decided to grab an apple from the breakfast room and head for Heathrow. He knew he would arrive at the airport well before Traci's plane landed; but he wanted to cover all absurd contingencies, any lengthy delays, or her flight arriving early.

They had arranged to meet in Terminal One greeting area, a place where Bryce could have coffee, read a newspaper and keep his eye on the large 'arrivals' board. When he saw Aer Lingus 34 was on the ground, he began pacing. Twenty minutes later Traci came through the automatic door.

He saw her first, before she spotted him and was surprised to feel he was meeting an old friend rather than someone he had just met. He watched her shiny red hair bounce as she walked with a determined stride. She was wearing the simple but stylish beige dress she had worn on the flight from San Francisco. But something in her manner was different. As he moved quickly toward her, she spotted him and stepped up her pace pulling the roller bag behind.

Instinctively he opened his arms and gave her a hug. He sensed tightness in her shoulders. Neither spoke. Bryce knew when she was ready to talk, she would. The agenda was hers. She was visibly stressed and obviously fatigued. A quick glance revealed her wedding ring was missing. After returning his strong hug, she stepped back and forced a smile.

"I'll bet you're really glad to see me, huh?" Close up, he saw evidence of tears, a smearing of mascara on her cheek. "If you'll guard my bag, I'll find a lady's room and see if I can repair this mess."

While Traci was away Bryce looked at her suitcase ID tag. Traci Dunne/9165 #7 Bridgeview Drive/Sausalito CA 94965.

"Can I spring for a cab?" asked a much-improved Traci Dunne from Sausalito when she returned.

"Cabs are too slow, and expensive," Bryce answered. "Besides, you need to see how easy it is to get around here on public transportation. Let me be the teacher and give you a lesson on train travel."

Whatever the source of stress, Traci seemed to be recovering, at least for the moment. Glad for Bryce's help, she answered with, "I'm up for that. Teach away."

Buying Traci a Three Day Travel Card and following the Underground route Bryce had taken two days before, they headed for the Marble Arch station. Along the way, responding to Traci's question, "What have you been up to since I saw you last?" Bryce talked about the self-guided walking tour and his trip to Bath. She was especially interested in knowing about Bath Abbey.

"The official name is the Abbey of St. Peter and St. Paul," Bryce explained. "The building went through a number of changes due to neglect, fire and turf battles. In the early centuries, before the Reformation, it served as a Benedictine monastery. Now it's an Anglican parish and a magnificent gothic cathedral. It's a great place to visit."

"Maybe I'll do that sometime."

The staff of the Edward Lear displayed their normal graciousness in welcoming Traci. She was given a key to her room and the hotel's entry door with the admonition to take the keys with her when she goes out because the entry door is always locked. She was shown the location of the breakfast room and the library where the Wi-Fi Internet computer was available.

Traci suggested she needed to rest a couple of hours then go with Bryce someplace quiet to talk and maybe have an early dinner.

They agreed to meet in the hotel's library at four. Bryce did a walkabout of the neighborhood to scout out a restaurant where they could have a good meal and, hopefully, a quiet conversation. He selected the tea room at the four-star Rubens Hotel with its classic understated ambience and secluded tables.

When he returned to the Edward Lear library he logged online to see if there were messages from his office. There was only one. It was from Sharon, his administrative assistant.

As much as I know you will hate to hear it, the office is running very smoothly without you. Please continue having a pleasant journey. Maintain the phoning schedule we set up, as I know you just can't stand not hearing my drill-sergeant voice.

Bryce moved away from the computer, sat in a large overstuffed leather chair, stretched his legs and put his feet on an ottoman in front of the chair. He quickly dozed off.

———————

"Hey, wake up, the day's just beginning."

Bryce smiled at the sound of Traci's voice, but kept his eyes closed. When he slowly opened them, she was returning his smile.

She looked rested, refreshed and beautiful. She must have used the steam iron in her room; her beige dress had also been refreshed.

It was a mile or more walk to the Reubens Hotel where they would be dining, but Bryce picked that location for its proximity to Buckingham Palace as well as for the food. They could walk on over to Buckingham through Green Park on their way back to the Edward Lear.

Once seated in the restaurant and ordering a bottle of wine, the two sat in silence. After what seemed far too long to Bryce, Traci began.

"First of all, thank you for letting me intrude on your trip. I know how important this journey is to you. I'll not be in town for long, and I've no intent of slowing you down."

Bryce started to respond but Traci put up her hand, letting him know he needn't say anything.

"Please, just let me talk," she continued. "I really need to talk. I know how presumptuous this is of me; but at the moment I'm totally out of friends and I need someone I can talk to. This is very difficult, so I'll just babble on in a stream of consciousness hoping part of it makes sense."

She paused for a moment for a sip of wine. The tuxedoed waiter approached to take their dinner order but Bryce asked him to give them a little time.

"I told you I'm a school teacher; I just finished my eleventh year. I love teaching and everything about it, the children, the challenge and responsibility of molding young minds and instilling positive character traits that will lead to their becoming responsible adults. What I didn't tell you is...all my teaching experience has been in a Catholic diocese school system. I belong to an order of Religious Sisters whose mission is to provide service to schools, hospitals and social programs."

Bryce couldn't keep quiet. "You're a nun?" he blurted.

"No, not technically. Members of the sisterhood do take vows of chastity and fidelity, but don't take the Vow of Enclosure. I wore a wedding ring to signify I was a 'bride of Christ'. I know all of this seems very mysterious. But please, please let me finish."

"Okay, sorry."

"I mentioned my father and his religious zeal. It was his goal, from the time Michael and I were born, for the two of us to be totally involved in the church. From kindergarten through college we were immersed in catechism and raised under the strict discipline of Catholicism. Living in Philadelphia, I attended St. Leonard's Academy, an all-girls prep school, then to Immaculata, an all-women's college, for my undergraduate degree. For a time after graduation I worked for my father in his Guinness distributorship before deciding to join the order. When I took my vows and chose teaching as my vocation, I attended Villanova University to get my teaching credentials.

"My decision was made after a great deal of thought. My father was pleased and proud that both his children were devoting their lives to the work of the church. We added to his bragging pool. I was devastated when he passed away so quickly, three years ago. I loved him dearly; but after a while I began to realize his death brought with it a sense of freedom I'd never had. Not that it made any difference to my commitment to the church or my students. When my mother died, I felt I had lost my best friend. I didn't feel alone, just lonely.

"You aren't given the opportunity to make many close friends when you choose a spiritual life over a secular one. There were only four members of my order teaching at our school. We shared two apartments in a small building owned by the diocese within walking distance of the school. Most of our social life revolved around doing things with the school or our local parish."

"I'm curious," Bryce interjected. "You keep referring to these things in past tense."

"Yes, I'll get to that soon. Like all schools, we counted on a lot of volunteer help in our classrooms. Parents or other relatives would come on a scheduled basis to grade papers, tutor children who needed help with reading or math or chaperone field trips. Most of the volunteers were good, well meaning people. I ended up with one who proved to be a real jerk.

"Does the name Clifton Norton mean anything to you?"

"If he's the Clifton Norton who's CEO of Norton Enterprises, it sure does. He's quite the philanthropist. Seems like his picture is in the newspaper at least once a month showing him attending some charitable fund raising event. Lauren served with his wife as an advisor to a County commission dealing with family and children's issues. I met him once at a dinner meeting."

"He's the one all right. In addition to everything else, he's the president of our diocese school board. Last winter my class and

I presented a program for the board at one of their monthly meetings. The children did a wonderful job and got a standing ovation from the board members and people in the audience.

"At the end of the meeting, Mr. Norton came to me expressing his appreciation, on behalf of the board, for our program. A couple of weeks later he showed up in my classroom at the end of the school day and asked about volunteering. He said he had a very busy schedule but he could clear time one afternoon a week.

"Of course, I was thrilled. What a perfect role model of success for my kids. For five or six weeks he came by, always at the end of the day. I gave him papers to grade, pencils to sharpen and work folders to assemble. Then he told me he had an idea for a teaching unit on how businesses operate. While I thought this was a little advanced for seven-year-olds, he assured me he could pitch the presentation to their level of understanding.

"When he supposedly had the PowerPoint presentation of the unit ready, he suggested we meet in his office after hours to review it. He sent a car to the apartment to pick me up – much to the curiosity of my roommate, Sister Barbara."

"Oh, my gosh," Bryce said. "I can see where this is headed."

"Unfortunately, I couldn't," Traci lamented. "When I got to his office, everyone had left for the day. A table was filled with hors d'oeuvres and champagne was chilling in a silver ice bucket. A bottle of Scotch was on his desk. It was obvious by his actions he had been drinking. When he locked the office door, I became frightened.

"He said very disturbing things. I was so sexy and beautiful; his wife didn't understand his needs; he had been attracted to me from the minute he met me; he knew how to show a woman a good time. He tried to give me a diamond bracelet. I refused and he became belligerent. He started pawing at me. I thought I was going to be molested so I slapped at him and screamed for help. This backed him down and he staggered to the door and unlocked it. I'll never forget the look in his eyes. I ran from the building and hailed a cab to get home. Fortunately, Sister Barbara was out so I had a chance to settle down. I was really shaken."

"I hope you blew the whistle on the bastard," Bryce said sternly.

"This happened on a Friday. I used the weekend to consider what I should do. I didn't even go to mass for fear of running into him. My decision was to have a private audience with our Mother Superior before doing anything else. When I got to work on Monday morning I was met by our principal who told me I was to go into a meeting before school started. I went to the conference room where I was greeted by the Bishop, Mother Superior and the superintendent of the diocese schools. They informed me a complaint had been filed by Mr. Norton alleging I was an immoral woman who should not be teaching children.

"He totally reversed the scenario from Friday. His story was he invited me to his office to review a PowerPoint presentation he had prepared for my class. I arrived, apparently inebriated, and made moves on him that were embarrassing. My physical advances and lurid behavior left him no choice but to ask me to leave."

"And they bought that crock?" Bryce asked, his anger growing.

"It really didn't matter who did or didn't. Norton is the president of the school board and for years has pledged large sums of money to the school and church. Sometimes Goliath wins. My teaching contract was terminated – for cause – and I was given 72 hours to vacate my apartment. I found myself without a job, without a home and without transportation. I was shaken to the core. Then I remembered something my father told me when I was young, 'Teresa Roisin, my love, it's not what others think of you that matters – it's what you think of yourself.' That put things in a better perspective, but I was so hurt.

"I wanted to run away, to leave that terrible place and that terrible man. That's when I decided to visit Michael, who has always been there for me; my friend and confidant. I had put away some money I had received from my parent's inheritance so I took some of that and bought a car, leased an apartment, rented a postal box to receive my forwarded mail, left a form with the post office directing it to hold my mail until I return from my trip and made an airline reservation, all within 72 hours. Not bad, huh?"

"Not bad at all," Bryce replied. "But it seems not all went well for you with Michael. Or am I jumping ahead?"

"My short time with him was disappointing to say the least. A side of him I hadn't seen before showed itself. I was hoping for his support, his understanding of the unfairness of the situation. I wanted him to do battle with the powers that be, put on the armor of righteousness; climb on his trusty steed and like St. George ride off to slay the dragons. Instead, his advice was to not rock the boat. Oh, he believed my version of the story without question. But he's in line for a prominent position in a New Jersey diocese and didn't want to do anything to jeopardize that possibility. His attitude made me so angry I yelled at him and took off my ring. I left his house and took a taxi the 40 miles back to the Dublin airport."

"Wow!" Bryce said. "You're quite a woman."

Then he added wryly, "What you need is a lawyer. I have a very good one in mind I'd like to recommend."

CHAPTER FOUR

BRYCE and Traci talked for another hour over dinner, changing the conversation to more lighthearted subjects, starting with childhood memories. Bryce shared the early years with his mother, his good fortune to be adopted by the Gibsons and how it was – by their support and encouragement – he decided to become a lawyer.

Traci wondered aloud how her life might have been different if she had attended public school. She had been envious of other girls who were invited to proms, of being able to go out on Friday nights and cheer for a football team, of being in school drama where girls didn't have to play the male roles.

Lauren came into the conversation on many topics. Bryce marveled how two people as totally opposite as they could share so much fun and happiness together. Bryce had a photo album of Lauren in his room; Traci said she would like to see it. She was curious to see pictures of the woman she had heard so much about.

At the hotel, the two said goodnight with an agreement to meet in the hotel library at eight o'clock the next morning and have breakfast together.

————————————

Traci appeared promptly at eight to find Bryce reading the morning paper.

"Good morning," he said cheerfully. "I was checking to see what might be playing on stage. There is always good theater in London."

"What did you find?"

"There are two still running Lauren and I saw: Phantom of the Opera and The Lion King. They're both excellent and well worth seeing again. Would you be interested in going with me? I'll see if tickets are available."

"Sounds great. I saw Phantom when the touring company came

to San Francisco."

"Then Lion King it is."

The breakfast room was bustling with activity but a couple was leaving one of the two-person tables and they headed for it. The Scotsman, engrossed in conversation with the others at his table, stopped to give Bryce two-thumbs-up approval on his breakfast companion.

Bryce ordered the full Monty; Traci settled for eggs and bacon.

"I've given a lot of thought about our talk last night," Bryce said. "From my perspective, it seems it would be in your best interest to let me pursue some possible legal action on your behalf. We may not be able to get your job reinstated but we can raise such a ruckus they'll think twice before hurting anyone else."

"I was hoping to talk about possibilities. I agree whole-heartedly. I would appreciate your working with me, even if it's for nothing more than reclaiming my good reputation."

"Let's do it. For this worthy cause, I'll work the case pro bono."

"Absolutely not! How would that come across? I'm already accused of plying my wiles on one man. I don't want you added to the list. My father established a trust in his will leaving me a great deal of money. I'll have no problem paying your fee."

"Okay, I surrender," Bryce said, holding his hands in the air. "I think I just witnessed an example of 'getting your Irish up'."

"Where do we start?" Traci asked, flashing her trademark smile.

"We start by putting the fear of the Lord into them. Do you have a private email account or did you do everything through the school?"

"I have one, but seldom use it."

"Who is the highest authority in the church with knowledge of the situation?"

"Bishop Grogan was in the meeting when I was fired."

"Then here's the first step: I'll draft a letter from you to the Bishop informing him you have legal counsel to represent you in a potential lawsuit against the diocese for breach of contract. We'll say quite a bit more as well. Then we let him stew in that juice for a while."

"For how long?"

"Until we get back to San Francisco. The letter will reference the fact you're out of the country and unreachable for an unspecified period of time."

Traci sat quietly for a while, and then spoke.

"I'm feeling a little apprehensive at the moment. I'm very relieved to have a tentative plan for redeeming my reputation but I'm thinking a law suit might be a little too much."

"You're the one to make that decision," Bryce answered.

Traci again sat quietly, staring at her folded hands.

"Okay, counselor," Traci finally sighed. "We'll go for it. The letter should be signed 'Sister Teresa Dunne'. Some people think 'Traci' is too cutesy, so at school I'm 'Teresa'. But you said, 'when we get back to San Francisco'. Don't you mean, when you get back?"

"No, I meant we. I'm planning as I talk. I do that a lot. We're both here for different reasons. I'm expected to be gone for some weeks; you have no incentive to go back. I want to continue my 'sentimental journey' and you've never been to Europe.

"Preparing a lawsuit requires a lot of time between lawyer and client. If you tag along with me, you'll see a great deal of Europe and we'll have an airtight brief ready to file when we get back."

Once again, Traci contemplated before responding.

"That makes sense," Traci said finally. "What do I need to do?"

"I mentioned I have a 90-day Eurail pass. You can only get these in the U.S. before your European travel begins. I'll have Sharon, my administrative assistant; place an expedited order in your name for a pass to be sent to my office. She can FedEx it overnight to the Edward Lear. I'll have her set up a client file and bill you for the price of the pass. We can go to the United Airlines office at Trafalgar Square to change your return ticket to open-ended."

"I'm totally unprepared for a trip," Traci said.

"I figured as much," Bryce replied. "Not to be critical, but you've worn the same dress every day."

"No, I really haven't," Traci chuckled. "My luggage wardrobe consists of 12 identical beige dresses. It's the uniform of my religious order."

"Then I know how we should spend today," Bryce announced. "Let's go shopping."

———————

For one-stop shopping in London you need look no farther than Harrods. Since the store first opened its doors as a grocery on

London's East End in 1849, Harrods has prided itself in excellent customer service and excellent merchandise. To escape the press of the inner city and to capitalize on trade to the Great Exhibition of 1851 held in Hyde Park, the store moved to its current location in the new district of Knightsbridge. The store's motto of "All Things for All People, Everywhere" says it well.

The tenacity of the founders was no better displayed than in early December 1883 when the store burned to the ground. In the face of unbelievable odds, all of the pre-Christmas orders were delivered on time and made a record profit for the store.

Lauren loved Harrods. She loved its history and walking the same isles as Noel Coward, Sigmund Freud, Oscar Wilde, Queen Mary, A. A. Milne and her favorite movie star, Pierce Bronson was thrilling.

Yet, for all that, her last journal entry regarding Harrods read, *On to Harrods and through all the grand rooms and finally to the Food Court – to discover in the Bread and Bakery room a long line queued up for...Krispy Kreme doughnuts! Oh dear, Starbuck's and Krispy Kreme! What is happening to London town?*

The sun reflected brightly onto the display windows of Harrods as Bryce and Traci came to the street surface from the Knightsbridge tube station. The large green awnings with the trademark "H" provided some relief from the glare.

Entering Harrods for the first time is a visual – if not intimidating – treat. Traci stood just inside the door, awestruck by the store's size and studied layout.

"This will be a very long day," she confessed to Bryce. "There's a lot more here than I'm used to seeing in our local Ross store."

"Take all the time you need," Bryce said. "My best advice is something I learned from Lauren. Look for outfits that will give a good ensemble combination. For example, one pair of black slacks and one pair of tan or white will let you have any number of blouse or shirt choices. Select lightweight, wrinkle-resistant items that can be rolled tightly for packing.

"Lauren was fond of saying, 'there are two kinds of travelers: those who pack lightly and those who wish they had'. Find some comfortable walking shoes. I'll stay with you if you like. Otherwise, I'll go back to the hotel and get to work."

"I'll be just fine. I have my pass and a tube map. I won't get too lost."

Bryce was still working at the computer in the hotel library when Traci returned from shopping, two Harrods' bags in each hand.

"How did you do?" he asked.

"Fairly well I think. Having lived a very disciplined life was a big help, otherwise I'd still be in that fabulous store maxing out my credit card. How about you?"

"I've managed to get started. I emailed the office asking Sharon to set up your account and order the Eurail pass. London is ten hours ahead of San Francisco, so she'll be getting to work in a couple of hours. She'll let me know when the ball is rolling. Also, I drafted a letter for you to send to Bishop Grogan. As soon as you approve, we can ship it off by email. Oh, yes! Not all business. On the way back from Harrods I stopped by a theater ticket outlet and got Lion King seats for tonight's show."

"Stop, you're wearing me out," Traci laughed. Then added, "I'll go freshen up and try on some of my new clothes. What's your plan for dinner?"

"Do you like sushi?"

"Love it."

"There's a very nice Japanese restaurant on Bond Street, not far from here. The food is great and the service quick. Let's give it a try on the way to the theater. I'll bring along copies of the Grogan letter to discuss while eating. The show is at eight. Would meeting back here in two hours give enough time for you to do your thing?"

"Perfect. See you in a couple."

————————

Bryce was already in the library printing copies of the Grogan letter when Traci stepped into the room and cleared her throat for attention. Bryce turned to see her assuming the pose of a professional model, then striding with flair around the room. She was stunning, dressed in black pants and white Marrakesh tunic.

"Our lightweight tunics add sophisticated style without adding weight to your bag or taking a toll on your budget," Traci announced in an exaggerated runway announcer's tone. "Our tunics are made of machine-washable polyester. Packing pouch is included.

"Our pants go from party to party without any stops at the dry cleaner. Naturally forgiving, thanks to the fabric's inherent stretch, they also feature back elastic, an invisible side zipper, and front darts for gentle shaping.

"Our Dansko shoes have long been known for comfort. But now, thanks to new materials, they're also marvelously lightweight and easy to pack."

She then performed a graceful toe-swirl and ended with a Peter Pan stance, hands on hips.

"My gosh! I'm speechless," Bryce was finally able to sputter.

"Now there's a first; a lawyer with nothing to say. Let's go eat."

As their dinner was being prepared, Bryce pulled from his pocket the folded drafts of the letter to Bishop Grogan. They both read their copy silently.

Bishop Grogan,

This is a courtesy notice of my intent to bring legal action against you, the diocese and my former school, citing the following reasons:

My contract was egregiously terminated based on a spiteful and unsubstantiated lie. This was allowed to happen with no regard for my stellar performance reviews over many years of dedicated service or my testimony regarding the named circumstances.

The timing and conditions of my termination have caused me great anguish and mental turmoil. Being summarily dismissed without an opportunity to see my students to say goodbye or express how much I love them is unconscionable.

The 72 hour eviction notice from my apartment violates city, county and state regulations.

I have retained a San Francisco law firm to represent me in this matter. I am out of the country now, and will be for some time. I simply had to get away and seek God's healing grace.

My faith in my God and my Church remains strong and unfaltering. My faith in some who claim to be His servants does not.

When I return you will receive the official complaint from the Court, as filed by my law firm.

With sincere regret and determined resolve,

Sister Teresa Dunne

When she finished reading the draft, she let out a slow whistle before rereading the letter.

"Well?" Bryce asked, "What do you think?"

"I think I'm sure glad I have a lawyer. You show a constraint I couldn't have managed. I wouldn't have known how or where to begin. I do have a question, though. There's no mention of Clifton

Norton. Does he get a free pass?"

"No way! We'll be building our case against him from the ground up. First, we make the Bishop pee himself, knowing he'll get others in the school and church involved so they can prepare for what's going to come down on them. I have a hunch a lot of panic will run through their sanctimonious veins, looking for a way out.

"They know full well who got them into this pickle. When Norton isn't mentioned in your letter, it will look like he isn't going to be implicated. They will rant as to the unfairness of it all. Of course, they'll look to him for direction but, like Pilate, he'll wash his hands of the whole mess. They'll be left alone to deal with us regarding the unfair termination and illegal eviction, for which we'll be asking a healthy compensation settlement.

"When that's over and done with, we'll hit Norton with a defamation of character law suit and charge him with leading a conspiracy to defame; the coconspirators having already been through the wringer once. We'll get the letter off to the Bishop in the morning, before we head for Windsor."

"Whoa, we're going to Windsor tomorrow?"

"That's on my schedule. I'd love to have you come along. But for now, let's find The Lion King and enjoy the genius of Sir Elton John."

CHAPTER FIVE

To get an early start on the day, Bryce and Traci agreed to meet in the hotel library at seven. They would send the Bishop Grogan email, head to Victoria Station for a quick breakfast and then take the Green Line bus to Windsor on its 9:15 run. Traci arrived downstairs wearing another Harrods ensemble.

"For a woman who's lived the simple life, you sure know how to spruce up," Bryce greeted her.

"My life wasn't always so simple," she replied pleasantly. "But thanks for the compliment. Before we leave England, I'd like to find a thrift store and donate a dozen beige dresses."

After their second trip to England – which included an outing to Windsor – Lauren made it clear to Bryce she would like to visit this rural wonderland whenever they were nearby. Her journal entry expressed this.

I love Windsor and all it represents: the history, the pageantry, and the excesses. Today the Queen's standard was flying above the castle announcing to the world she was somewhere inside that magnificent structure, the largest castle in all of Europe. We visited the State Apartments (I kept a sharp watch for Elizabeth, but didn't spot her), and the extraordinarily detailed Queen Mary's Dolls' House.

Our last stop inside the castle grounds was St. George's Chapel, resplendent with its tombs and crypts. An organist was rehearsing for an upcoming concert, so we sat and drank in the glorious sounds of Beethoven. I closed my eyes and imagined we were sitting in our pew on the day those pipes sounded their first notes. Perfect timing to be there at this moment!

Leaving the Castle grounds, through a portion of Windsor Village, we walked down the hill and over the river to Eton and strolled along the main street fronted by Eton College. Bryce bought a leather change purse with the Eton College emblem in gold as a souvenir.

We learned Eton was founded in 1440 by King Henry VI. As a college art minor, I was interested to discover the Eton chapel to be a fine example of 15th-century Perpendicular style architecture similar to King's College Chapel in Cambridge where we visited last year.

A wonderful, wonderful day!

The Queen's standard wasn't flying over the castle when Bryce and Traci arrived in Windsor, prompting Traci to quip, "Well, if we plan to see the Queen, I guess we'll have to settle for a visit to Buckingham."

The remainder of the day was reminiscent of the times Bryce and Lauren were at Windsor. Twinges of sadness pricked Bryce occasionally, but he held those moments in check. Traci was impressed with St. George's chapel, remembering it was the wedding venue of Prince Charles and Camilla.

Walking down the hill from the chapel to Eton, Traci had asked Bryce, "Are you a religious person?"

"Perhaps you should define religion. I went to Sunday school as a kid and church camps in summers and was involved a lot with the youth group in our church when I was in high school. Does that count?"

"I mean, do you believe in God? Or any other form of Supreme Being? Do you think the Earth was created by some big bang out there in infinity or was it shaped and molded by a superior intelligence? Are you a creationist or an evolutionist? What about Heaven and hell?"

"Hey, one thing at a time," Bryce pleaded. "I've never been cross examined on those issues before. I'm sure I have an opinion stored somewhere in my brain, but these are pretty heavy-duty questions.

"Do I believe in God? Yes. But I have a hard time understanding how He, or She, operates sometimes. For instance, how does God make a decision when two people are sincerely praying for things entirely opposite? When half the family prays for grandma to recover from her stroke and the other half prays for her to pass on so her suffering will end; when a man works hard all his life and prays to God every day for just one small financial break that never comes; when around-the-world prayer chains implore God's mercy to intercede in the starvation deaths of millions of children dying in Darfur and they keep dying? It could be George Clooney is doing more than God for those poor souls."

Traci was moved by Bryce's response. "There are some mysteries none of us will have answered satisfactorily," Traci said. "So, are you angry at God?"

"No, Sister, not angry just disappointed. I can remember as a kid I'd pray once in a while. Kid things, like hitting a homerun playing baseball or for a bad snowstorm so school would be cancelled. As an adult, I've prayed exactly three times. The first two were during Lauren's miscarriages. I prayed the best I knew how in hopes of saving both Lauren and the babies. Lauren lived, the babies didn't. The third – and last – time I prayed was for Lauren to recover from her accident. So I guess, if I'm keeping score, it's two out of five. If you don't mind waiting for my thoughts on evolution and life-after-death, I really do need time to think those through."

"I don't mind waiting," Traci said encouragingly. "Not at all."

On the return trip to Victoria Station, they agreed their time in Windsor was fun and interesting. On their way from Marble Arch to the hotel they stopped at Spencer & Marks to create carryout salads and select a bottle of wine. After freshening up from the trip, they would have dinner in Hyde Park.

Before returning to their rooms for the night, Bryce checked email. Two positive things had occurred. Sharon reported Traci's Eurail pass had been expedited. The "read message" receipt Traci requested when sending her letter to Bishop Grogan was received. All systems were go.

By the time the two met for breakfast, Bryce had scheduled the day's itinerary. They would take the tube to the Tower Bridge and walk across to the Tower of London. After visiting the Tower they would board a sightseeing boat at the Tower Pier and cruise the River Thames to Westminster Pier, disembark and walk past the Houses of Parliament – listening for Big Ben to strike on the hour – and on to Westminster Abbey. After absorbing the history and grandeur of the Abbey, it's a walk across Westminster Bridge to the Jubilee gardens for a flight on the London Eye.

Traci wanted to attend mass in the evening. Bryce recalled when he and Lauren had spent time exploring Covent Gardens they had looked inside a small Catholic church. Bryce referred to Lauren's journal and found the name and location: Crusader

House on St. John's Street. This would be their last stop before returning to the hotel.

From his early days as a history buff, the Tower of London had fascinated Bryce. When he finally got to see it, he was hooked for good. Her Majesty's Royal Palace and Fortress – the Tower's formal name – is located on the north bank of the Thames River. The Tower is a stark square fortress built by William the Conqueror in 1078. The Tower as a whole, however, is made up of several separate buildings within two rings of defensive walls and a moat.

Through the centuries the Tower has functioned as a fortress, a royal palace, a prison, a torture chamber, a place of execution, an armory, a treasury, a zoo, the Royal Mint, a public records office, an observatory, and – since 1303 – the home of the Crown Jewels of the United Kingdom.

The list of persons incarcerated in the Tower is long and impressive, beginning with the first prisoner, Bishop Ranulf Flambard of Durham who, in 1100, was found guilty of extortion. Other prominent inmates included John Balliol, King of Scotland, King David II of Scotland, King John II of France, Henry Laurens (third President of the Continental Congress of Colonial America), Sir Thomas More (executed), King Henry VI of England (murdered), King Edward V of England and his brother Richard, Sir Walter Raleigh (for 13 years), Guy Fawkes, Lord George Gordon, and – in more modern times – Rudolf Hess (deputy leader of the German Nazi Party in 1941).

While lower-class criminals were usually executed by hanging at one of the public execution sites outside the Tower, high-profile convicts, such as Sir Thomas More were publicly beheaded on Tower Green and buried in the Chapel Royal of St. Peter, next to the Green.

Seven persons found guilty of treason, five of them women, were beheaded on the Tower Green: William Hastings, Anne Boleyn, Margaret Pole, Catherine Howard, Jayne Boleyn, Lady Jane Grey and Robert Devereux.

The last person executed in the Tower was German spy Josef Jakobs, by a firing squad formed from the Scots Guards in 1941.

As much as Bryce reveled in the history of the White Tower, so Lauren enjoyed the grandeur of Jewel House. She wrote in her journal:

The biggest draw for me to keep returning to the Tower of Lon-

don is the Jewel House. Maybe it's because I played make-believe Queen when I was little. I would dress my dolls in velvet robes and pretend they were my princesses. What a wonderful surprise it was the first time I saw the real Crown Jewels. The ten crowns (one with the famous Koh-i-Noor diamond), the scepters (especially the one with the biggest cut diamond in the world, the 350-carat Star of Africa), the jeweled swords, the Orb are all so very - very. Big bummer though – no picture taking is allowed.

"I'm sorry to rush us through in just two hours," Bryce apologized as they left the Tower to walk to the Thames for the boat cruise. "Just consider this trip through Europe to be your 'Whitman Sampler'."

It was early evening by the time they visited Westminster Abbey and had their London Eye adventure, but they made it to Covent Gardens in time to experience some of the hustle and bustle before reaching Crusader House for six o'clock mass. Bryce hesitated at the door.

"You go on in," he said to Traci. "I'll wait out here."

"Why?"

"No reason. I thought maybe you'd like some quiet time alone to, you know, do whatever you folks do in there."

"There's really nothing dark or mysterious behind this door. It's very similar to most church services. Maybe a little more structured. Scripture is read from both the Old and New Testaments; the liturgy of the week is followed – with the congregation participating; then the priest does a homily, or sermon. At the end, communion is offered, but not everyone takes it."

"What about confession, going into the closet with the curtains pulled to tell the priest your sins?" Bryce asked. "I wouldn't feel comfortable doing that."

"Confession isn't a part of mass," Traci laughed. "Priests have scheduled times to hear confessions. Come on, be bold."

———————————

They decided to return to the hotel by way of Trafalgar Square to change Traci's airline ticket at United's office there, and then go on to Piccadilly Circus.

"There is so much to do and see in this city," Traci marveled. "I think I'd enjoy living here if I could ever get used to all the taxis and busses coming along on the wrong side of the street."

"Any thoughts about what you would like to see tomorrow?" Bryce asked.

"St. Paul's Cathedral is a must. In college, I did a term paper on Christopher Wren and the rebuilding of the cathedral after the great fire of London. Going to the British Museum and seeing the Rosetta Stone would be nice."

Bryce readily agreed.

"But it's not about me," Traci said. "This is your trip, your sentimental journey. It took me three months to get the hang of BART, but I'm learning the ropes on how to get around London very quickly, thanks to you. No need for me to be in your pocket every minute."

"Thanks, I appreciate that," Bryce replied. "I'm not much for museums a second time. Lauren never got enough of them. Her favorites were the Victoria and Albert and the Tate Modern Art Gallery. The Tate is very close to Shakespeare's Globe Theater and they're both in the vicinity of St. Paul's."

"Great," Traci said. "We have options."

Street musicians were performing all around Piccadilly Circus, and they stopped to listen to a few. Traci bought a CD from one group she especially liked, six elderly men from Ukraine playing gypsy music.

"What kind of music do you like?" she asked Bryce as he moved his body from side to side listening to a quartet reprising the Beatles' Penny Lane.

"Just about everything but grunge. Seattle, where I grew up, produced some pretty talented musicians, including Kurt Cobain, the creator of grunge. Jimi Hendrix was born there, the Brothers Four got their start at the University of Washington, and Kenny G graduated from my high school. Quincy Jones' family moved to Seattle from Chicago when Quincy was ten. Ray Charles came to town often. I have a vivid memory of him coming to one of our school assemblies. He sang and played his incredible piano and talked to us kids like we were special. The thing that stuck with me the most was his encouraging all of us to get involved with music. 'Play an instrument if you can; listen and enjoy if you can't.' He spoke directly to the kids in the audience who played the piano, encouraging them to learn classical pieces before they tried popular."

"Do you play an instrument?" Traci asked.

"No," Bryce laughed. "I had a promising career as a musician in the first and second grades. I played sticks in the rhythm band. I really got the knack of it in the first grade and by second grade I was first-chair in the stick section. Unfortunately, in third grade, we all had to learn to play something called a flute-a-phone which required reading music. The only thing I could manage was remembering the lines are Every Good Boy Does Fine and the spaces are FACE.

"The odd thing is, I can't read music but I can sing almost anything by ear once I've heard a song. In high school I sang solos, was in a barbershop quartet and a member of the all-state chorus. How about you? Do you play?"

"Yes, I know how to play; but I haven't in years," Traci confessed. "My father loved Irish music. Two of the favorite instruments in Ireland are accordion and fiddle, played as duets. At age seven I began accordion lessons and stayed with them through high school. Michael learned to fiddle. We were pretty good. My father threw a lot of parties at our house so we could be showcased."

"Why did you stop playing?" Bryce wanted to know.

"When Michael went away to seminary, the novelty wore off. Accordionists aren't much in demand, unless you're Myron Florin."

"Do you like to dance?" Bryce asked.

"Love it. I had both tap and ballet lessons. I learned tap so I could do Irish jigs and polkas. My mother encouraged me in ballet. When I was 12 I created a dance I called the Nutcracker Polka, combining the two. It was a hoot."

"What about ballroom dancing? I do a mean tango. I'm almost as good as Al Pacino was in Scent of a Woman."

"We had ballroom classes at St. Leonard's, but because there were no boys in our school I always had to lead. I'm more comfortable with what I call 'regular dancing' where you just get on the dance floor and move with the music."

For dinner, they decided on a takeout meal from the Piccadilly Pizza Hut and walked to a small park nearby. Scores of pigeons, looking for a handout, hopped around the bench where the two sat.

"Have you ever seen a dead pigeon?" Bryce asked. "Everywhere I go, there are pigeons – hundreds of them – but I've never seen a dead one."

"Maybe they know when their time is up and they go to some

secret dying place," Traci offered. "They're trying to be environ-
mentally friendly."

After eating and tossing crumbs to the pigeons, Traci made a request.

"Will you sing something? I'd like that."

"Do you mean here? Now?"

"Yes, please, if you don't mind."

"Okay, if you insist," Bryce smiled. "There's a song that runs
through my head every day. Sharon gave me a Willie Nelson CD
soon after Lauren was killed and I was in a real bad space. So
she suggested I listen to one of the cuts on the album whenever I
needed a promise for the future. The song is titled Healing Hands
of Time and has become my mantra for this chapter in my life."

They were still sitting in the park – people passing by – but everyone focused on their own thoughts. So Bryce cleared his throat,
took a deep breath, closed his eyes and began to sing.

> They're working while I'm missing you
> Those healing hands of time
> And soon they'll be dismissing you
> From this heart of mine
> They'll lead me safely through the night
> And I'll follow as though blind
> My future tightly clutched within
> Those healing hands of time
> They let me close my eyes just then
> Those healing hands of time
> And soon they'll let me sleep again
> Those healing hands of time
> So already I've reached mountain peaks
> And I've just begun to climb
> I'll get over you by clinging to
> Those healing hands of time

Bryce's voice trembled as he repeated the last stanza.

> I'll get over you by clinging to
> Those healing hands of time

Traci squeezed Bryce's arm tightly.

"Thank you," she said softly. "That was beautiful. I needed to
hear those words myself, more than you'll ever know."

CHAPTER SIX

BRYCE was restless on returning to his room. Not a bad state of mind, just reviewing the day and wondering what his tomorrow would bring. He pulled the photo album from his suitcase and slowly leafed through the pages. This was the first time he had felt strong enough to look at pictures of Lauren taken during their trips to Europe. From the hundreds he had at home to pick, he selected sixty to bring on the trip.

Each picture told a story. Bryce allowed his mind to wander back in time and space to be reminded of each event. All the photos showed a smiling Lauren, a happy and contented Lauren, a much-in-love Lauren.

Not that their trips didn't occasionally have a down side.

Once a professional thief entered their sleeping compartment when traveling by train somewhere between Nice and Marseilles in the middle of the night and snatched a bag containing their passports, Eurail passes, travelers' checks, cash and – important to Lauren – her makeup case. Fortunately, the thief was apprehended before he could get off the train. Bryce and Lauren spent the rest of the night in the police station of Nimes filing a complaint and giving a formal deposition to the French gendarmes against the crook.

On another memorable occasion, Bryce became very ill after leaving Stuttgart on the way to Zurich, resulting in leaving the train to find lodging in a small town and stay immobilized in a tiny hotel room until he recovered.

But the good times far outweighed the bad – until Lauren's death. Even so, Bryce was getting better in using the memory of the many fun trips to push the disastrous one further and further out of his mind.

He considered having met Traci to be fortuitous for them both. However, trying to put that chance meeting into an understandable perspective was not a simple exercise. If he were to read it in a novel, it probably would make more sense than acting it out in real life. It wasn't that Bryce needed to be alone as he traveled, but he wasn't consciously aware of that until he and Traci met. Traci needed someone to help her through her rough patch; she also needed a lawyer, but she wasn't aware of that until she and Bryce met.

Was their meeting serendipitous or providential? Is serendipity just chance or a gift from God?

If the FedEx delivery is on schedule, tomorrow could be their last full day in England. If so, taking Traci to see Buckingham Palace should be first thing in the morning. Then, while Traci does her museum absorption, Bryce could go to the Eurostar station and make reservations for Belgium.

With these thoughts, sleep finally arrived.

Traci was slow coming down for breakfast. Bryce was concerned and started for her room but she met him on the stairs.

"Sorry I'm late," she apologized. "I had a pretty rough night. I'm feeling better now. I must look like something the cat dragged in."

"Do you want to talk about it?"

"No. At least not now. Maybe someday, if I can make sense enough of it to be coherent, I'll be ready to talk."

After sitting down for breakfast, Bryce changed the subject.

"If Sharon's information is right, we should be getting your Eurail pass today. I think we can plan on that and leave for the Continent tomorrow. Are you game?"

"Only if you're ready to leave England. Have you done everything you wanted to do?"

"Pretty much. I'd considered a day-trip to Oxford and maybe spending a couple of days in the Cotswolds, but I can pick those up another time."

"OK, if that works for you. But let's have an understanding." Traci's demeanor became serious. "This is your trip. It's not to be our trip in any respect. You have a plan to go and do and revisit places that meant so much to you and Lauren. Don't change one day of that plan because of me or you'll really witness the full-blown definition of a woman with her Irish up. I haven't been anywhere, so if I tag along everyplace will be new and exciting and it would be great to have my own personal tour guide. But you need to go and do what you set out to do."

Bryce looked into Traci's emerald eyes and saw a spark of fire punctuating her words. He smiled. She smiled. They both knew – without saying – the message had been delivered and received.

———————————

Later in the morning, after a quick visit to Buckingham Palace, Traci was off on her own to sightsee. Bryce returned to the Edward Lear. Traci's admonition was clear. She knew the overall broad-brush itinerary Bryce had verbalized on the plane, but he had shared nothing specific regarding timelines.

Traci should have her own copy of the itinerary. In the hotel library, Bryce reviewed the hard copy taken from his briefcase and made some revisions. After a shortened stay in Bruges they would trade a day in Metz for one in Luxembourg; Salzburg and Florence got three days each as did Provence and Barcelona. From Barcelona they would head for the Basque country for two days.Paris, the final destination before returning to Heathrow for their return home, remained totally sacrosanct with ten days of visiting.

"If we're doing a 'Whitman's Sampler'", Bryce said aloud, slipping his flash drive into the computer to edit the stored itinerary and print copies, "we may as well get a big box."

The FedEx package arrived mid-afternoon. Bryce checked to assure Traci's Eurail pass was in order then left a message with the desk clerk to tell Traci he had gone to the Eurostar terminal. He made reservations to Brussels on the next day's noon train. The trip would take just an hour and 40 minutes by Eurostar. In Brussels they would validate their Eurail passes and take the 30-minute trip to Bruges, arriving there by three in the afternoon.

To be on the safe side of finding a place to stay, Bryce planned to email the two-star Hotel Van Eyck, located just a few blocks from the central Market Square. If that attempt was unsuccessful, on arrival in Bruges he would leave Traci at the train station guarding the luggage while he scouted around for lodging. This was an adventure he shared many times with Lauren; although she much preferred to have tourist offices – found in most stations – make a reservation for them, especially if bad weather or late hours figured in. For the most part, Lauren let Bryce do his thing without fussing too much.

It was almost six o'clock before Traci returned from her outing. She had a marvelous day, she announced, and bought a new memory card for her digital camera when her other one filled up before leaving St. Paul's. She had gotten lost only once, but not for long. She was so taken with everything she had forgotten to eat. She was famished.

Bryce suggested they take a taxi and return to the tea room at the Rubens Hotel where they dined Traci's first night in London. The restaurant's host greeted them with a warm smile and led them to the same table where they sat earlier. He motioned to the wine steward, who responded promptly, and soon they were enjoying a bottle of Taylor Fladgate ten-year-old tawny port.

Rather than ordering a full dinner, they opted for hearty hors d'oeuvres. A string quartet played softly from a corner of the room. A waiter came by, lighting candles on the tables before dimming the house lights. The two sat quietly for a long while, captivated by the moment. Then Traci spoke. "Tell me about Bruges."

"Ah, Bruges. Any attempt to describe Bruges would do it a grave injustice. It's a city of some 100,000 residents with about 20,000 living within a mile of the town square. It's one of the most beautiful cities in Europe, famed for its lace and native son, the artist Jan van Eyck. It has dikes and canals and windmills and the Church of Our Lady has as its centerpiece Michelangelo's Madonna and Child. Are you sure you still want to go?"

"Can we go tonight?" Traci asked lightly. "I'm not sure I can wait until tomorrow. Oh, just a minute; I'm not packed. If we plan to even make it tomorrow, I'd better get started."They waited to leave until the quartet announced they were taking a 15-minute break. As they passed the restaurant host, he said to Bryce, while looking at Traci, "You have a beautiful companion." Bryce smiled and nodded in agreement. Traci blushed demurely.

Storms rolled through the skies all night; bolts of lightning gave warning of loud thunder claps. Toward dawn the storms subsided but left behind a steady rainfall. Bryce decided it would be best to take a taxi to the Eurostar station, which was quite a concession. Taxis were anathema to Bryce, although he had no good explanation why. He preferred to walk from hotels to train stations, train stations to hotels unless the distance was too great. Lauren would dutifully transport the luggage in her taxi and patiently wait for Bryce to arrive at their hotel, or the train station. On rare occasions when friends traveled with them, the friends always shared the taxi with Lauren.

They arrived at the Eurostar station well ahead of the scheduled departure time and sat sipping coffee, waiting for the boarding announcement.

"I hope you're not claustrophobic," Bryce said. "We'll be in a tunnel for 38 minutes going under the English Channel at the Straits of Dover. It connects southeastern England with northern France, Brussels and Paris. The English call it the 'Chunnel' which is their nickname for 'The Channel Tunnel'. In French it's called le tunnel sous la Manche. It's the second longest rail tunnel in the world. There are two complete transportation tunnels in the Chunnel utilized by four different train systems. The one we'll be on – the Eurostar – is a high speed passenger service. At times we'll be booking along at 185 miles-per-hour. The Eurotunnel shuttle carries cars and vans in enclosed railcars that allow drivers to drive their vehicles on and off. There are also two Eurotunnel freight service trains. The Chunnel has been called the Seventh Wonder of the Modern World."

"I'm really glad we're going this route instead of flying," Traci said. "But, not to worry," she added, pulling the rosary from her windbreaker pocket. "I'll make sure we get through the tunnel okay."

By the time the Eurostar made its one scheduled stop in Lille before leaving France for Belgium, the rain had stopped and the sky showed patches of blue. When they arrived in Brussels, the city was basking in warm sunlight. It took only a few minutes for a railroad official to validate their Eurail passes before they boarded a train for Bruges.

CHAPTER SEVEN

ONE of the impressions striking a first-time visitor arriving by train to Bruges is the hundreds of rental bicycles standing in neat rows of racks near the large parking area outside the terminal. For bicycle enthusiasts, this flat land behind the dykes is a two-wheel paradise. On their second visit to Bruges, Lauren and Bryce spent a full day bicycling, joining an organized tour starting at Burg Square.

Lauren's journal captured the day.

We spent 2½ hours in the morning peddling down winding back streets, into old parishes, past windmills and medieval fortifications and along the canals. We stopped at a number of historical locations and monuments like the Beguinage and the Lake of Love, with ever so many swans, and made a pit stop at an outdoor café for a brew.

In the afternoon we headed out of the city and into the stunning Flanders countryside. It was an easy ride from Bruges to the historic town of Damme, once an outer harbor of Bruges and now a quaint market town. We marveled at the beauty of the Flemish Polders region as we cycled along peaceful canals. Back in Bruges, sitting in an outdoor café in Market Square, we rewarded ourselves with another beer and a big order of frites with the traditional Belgian condiment, mayonnaise.

It was total fun; but, Mercy, we'll be sore tomorrow!

"Well, Sister, here we are. What do you think so far?"

"So far, I really like it. Please don't call me 'Sister.' I'm not sure I am one anymore. But even so, it sounds too formal coming from you. Not that I'm keeping score, but you've only nouned me twice and both times it's been 'Sister.' If you choose not to call me 'Traci', then I would prefer 'Hey You' over 'Sister'."

"Hey You, I'm sorry. I'll try to do better." They both laughed.

Traci declined Bryce's invitation to join him for the mile walk from the terminal to the Hotel van Eyck. Before leaving on foot, Bryce walked Traci to the head of the taxi queue and gave the driver the hotel's address. Earlier Bryce had explained Bruges is a very tourist-friendly city, a vacation destination for many Brits. To be hired in any shop or store, applicants have to be fluent in Flemish, French and English.

"We're expected at the hotel; reservations are in both our names. The woman who runs the hotel is the owner and a gracious host-ess. Ask the driver to put our bags in the ante room just inside the entrance. There's no elevator, so I'll lug them up the stairs when I get there."

Bryce handed the driver a 20 euro bill and asked if that would cover Traci's fare and the tip. The driver's smile and nod indicated it would more than cover both.

It was a bittersweet stroll. The afternoon sun, accompanied by a cool breeze made for perfect weather. This had been a favorite route for Lauren and Bryce after returning from day trips on the train. Walking through King Albert City Park which lies between the station and the heart of the city, the historical city center rises up from the horizon – a picture-perfect scene.

Bruges is surrounded by nature – as a result of history – which is very special. Medieval cities needed to be fortified and defended. This was achieved by ramparts around the city, created by walling the city and digging canals. The canals still exist, as do the city gates and promenade walks. Swans, the motif of Bruges, are in abun-dance, swimming gracefully among the tour boats that offer visitors a close and personal view of homes and life-style from water level.

When approaching Bruges from any direction, the tower of Our Lady's Church, looming 403 feet from ground level, where Michel-angelo's Madonna is displayed, dominates the skyline.

What normally is a 20 minute walk from the station to the hotel turned into more than an hour. Bryce was reluctant for it to end. Lauren's presence was the strongest he had felt since he was in Bath many days before. However, he noticed one difference. The feeling she was actually present in some ethereal form was slowly transforming into just memories.

At the hotel, Bryce discovered the proprietress and Traci had al-ready taken the bags to their rooms. Bryce was told Traci felt the need for a nap and he should knock on her door when he arrived.

Bryce and the woman talked for awhile. She was very saddened to learn of Lauren's death. Bryce and Lauren stayed in the van Eyck on three of their visits to Bruges.

"Lauren was so happy, so full of fun," the woman remembered. "And the lady you are with now? Is she . . ."

"She's a friend," Bryce responded quickly. "Only a friend."

Their rooms were directly across from each other so rather than disturb Traci's nap Bryce left his door open while unpacking. During his walk from the station he had a thought about their pending lawsuit against the school. He pulled a pad from his briefcase, scribbled some notes, and became mildly amused thinking of the turmoil they must have created with the email to the Bishop.

He knew the strategy was sound. Textbook cat and mouse. Without doubt the Bishop had his lawyers on the job, but they could do little until the suit was filed and they read the bill of particulars. Muhammad Ali would have approved. "Float like a butterfly, sting like a bee."

In a short time Traci rapped on the open door.

"Glad to see you didn't get lost," she said, flashing her patented smile. "Ready to show me Bruges?"

"Sure am. Let's go to the Market and have some frites and a beer."

"Beer I know, but what are frites?"

"The Belgian version of French fries, except they're longer and thinner and served in something similar to a cone-shaped coffee filter. You top them with mayonnaise or catsup if you ask. They're eaten with a little plastic fork, never with fingers."

"I tried drinking beer in college," Traci said, wrinkling her nose. "I didn't like it – not even Guinness – much to the chagrin of my father."

"You might want to try again. Belgium brews more than 350 varieties; so you can drink a different beer every day for almost a year and never have the same one twice. Lauren much preferred wine over beer, except when here in Bruges. She discovered a Lambic Ale called 'Boon Faro' and took a liking to it, especially when eating frites."

"Paraphrasing an old saying, 'When in Belgium, do as the Belgium's do', seems to fit the occasion," Traci replied. "I'll have a go, but you may have to finish it."

———————————

Strolling from the hotel to the square, Traci was impressed by the layout of the buildings and the stunning architecture.

"How about another history lesson?" Traci asked. "This is a fascinating city center."

"I thought you'd never ask," Bryce smiled.

"The Bruges Market Square serves many purposes. Identified as the commercial medieval heart of the city, the Market has been free from motorized traffic since 1996. The square is dominated by Cloth Hall, over there to our left, and the 272-foot high Belfry tower to our right. The tower was originally built in 1240 but was destroyed by fire in 1280. At the time of the fire, four wings of the Cloth Hall existed, as did two square segments of the belfry. The present octagonal lantern was added to the tower when it was re-built in 1486."

"Did the tower have a function, or was it built just to provide ambience?" Traci asked.

"As in most cities in the Low Countries the belfry tower was the repository for the city's important documents. The best part for me is the towers were used as watchtowers, complete with hanging bells, each having a distinct sound and function – bells for danger, bells for important announcements, and bells for indicating time. Later today, the belfry tower will charm us with a lovely 47 bell carillon. By the way, our hotel was built as a private mansion in 1700 or so."

Moving toward the center of the square, Traci was intrigued by the statues of two men.

"Those guys are Jan Breydel and Pieter de Coninck who led the Battle of the Golden Spurs – an uprising of the Flemish against the occupation of the French king – which took place in 1302," Bryce offered without being asked.

Bryce, being a history buff, thoroughly enjoyed researching most of the destinations before, during, and after trips with Lauren. She jokingly referred to him as "my living, breathing, talking travelogue."

Seated on one of the many benches forming a semi-circle around the base of the statue, Traci and Bryce speared mayonnaise covered frites with their little plastic forks and sipped beer from pint-sized paper steins. Nearby, the clip-clop of horses' hooves beat a steady rhythm as horse-drawn carriages arrived and departed the square.

"How's the beer?" Bryce asked. "Will there be any left for me?"

"It's really very good. With enough practice, I think I could become an occasional beer drinker."

"Did you hear that sound?" Bryce asked with feigned excitement. "That was your father rolling over in his grave."

When Traci returned from visiting the public restroom in the tower building, she asked, "Can we go to the Church of Our Lady and see the Madonna?"

"Of course; that's a great idea. And as we walk to the church we can take in some more history."

Standing in front of the masterpiece Bryce said, "Michelangelo sculpted this from Carrere marble in 1504 and it was the only one of his works to leave Italy in his lifetime. It was brought to Bruges by a local merchant, Jan van Moeskroen, and donated to the church in 1506."

"It's breathtaking," Traci commented softly. "I love this church. Think of the thousands and thousands of people from all over the world who have stood here feeling God's presence."

Traci slowly walked a few steps and turned a complete circle, looking at the ornate ceiling.

"Bryce, I'd like to stay a while. I'm feeling a little nostalgic. It's been some time since I visited the Stations of the Cross. I need to pray. You go ahead; I'll let you know when I'm back at the hotel."

"I'll be glad to wait."

"No, then I'd feel rushed. But thanks for the offer."

Bryce returned to the Market Square and had another beer. He'd felt for a couple of days something was troubling Traci, but didn't want to ask for an explanation. He was wishing he understood Catholicism better so he would have some idea what visiting the Stations of the Cross meant to a practicing Catholic.

Back in the room, he flipped on the television and found BBC playing old reruns of The Benny Hill Show. What a comic genius. They don't make them like that anymore. Benny Hill and Peter Sellers together would have made one hilarious combo in a television series.

In the middle of the second show, a rapping on the door roused Bryce from a light dozing.

"Bryce, I'm home. I'll see you in the morning. We can have breakfast. Good night."

"Good night, and sleep well."

———————

Another beautiful morning greeted the two as they left the hotel for the Square for a breakfast of Belgium waffles, eggs and sugar-cured ham. They decided this would be a lazy day of carriage and canal-boat rides, walking to the windmills and shopping for souvenirs. Traci appeared livelier than she had been the evening before.

"Glad to see you're more chipper this morning," Bryce said.

"Was it so obvious yesterday?" she asked.

"Yeah, there was something going on that didn't seem up to par."

"Sorry. I didn't mean to drag you down."

"No, no. It wasn't anything like that. Because you're so vivacious 95 percent of the time, the five percent slot becomes pretty apparent."

"Well, that was yesterday. Today is today, and I'll aim for the 100 percent score."

They chose to start by taking a horse-drawn carriage ride. The driver, a jolly round man with red cheeks and a floppy straw hat was also their guide. To the rhythm of the horse's trot through narrow streets and over small bridges he gave a running commentary of the historical significance of each major landmark they passed.

When they stopped to water the horse at the Beguinage, one of the typical areas in Bruges where one can find peace and quiet, the driver explained its history.

"The Beguinage of Bruges was founded in 1245 by the Countess of Flanders, the daughter of Count Baldwin who conquered Constantinople (now Istanbul) during the Crusades. In 1299, Philip the Beautiful of France placed the Beguinage under his rule. You may have noticed, when we entered over the bridge, the entrance gate bears the date 1776. Many of the houses here are much older. Most were built in the 17th and 18th centuries. Down there, at the end of that dead-end street you can find houses from the 15th and 16th centuries. The large house over in the corner behind the garden was where the 'grand-dame' lived. She was the boss of the place. In 1937 the Beguinage became a monastery for the Benedictine Sisters who still live here today."

"Would you like to come back here later and visit the Sisters?" Bryce asked jokingly.

"Only if they're serving Boon Faro ale and frites," Traci laughed.

The buggy ride was delightful. Then, after walking through winding residential streets and stopping for a sandwich, Traci and Bryce found their way to one of the five docks where people can board a canal boat. During their first visit to Bruges, Lauren expressed her reaction to the canal tour in her journal.

I've always felt the best way to explore new places is by walking, either free lance or following a printed walking tour guide. We spent our first two hours in Bruges doing just that: walking the main streets surrounding the Market Square. Then we decided to relax by taking a canal boat ride. We were pleasantly surprised. The boat took us to a number of extraordinary places we hadn't seen while walking. We would have missed so much of this lovely city if we hadn't taken the tour. Discovering where many of the beauty spots were hidden, we walked four more hours to explore further.

"What fun!" Traci said at the end of the half-hour ride.

Bryce was reflecting on his own wishes when he said, "Let's spend one more day here then head for Metz."

"That works for me," Traci agreed. "But there's so much to see here! So much to do!"

"More than we'll have time for. There are brochures in the hotel lobby, go through them tonight and pick the places you'd like see. One I can recommend is the Groeninge Museum which houses a collection of artworks spanning several centuries focusing mostly on painters who lived in Bruges."

"I'd like to visit another church," Traci said. "I've never seen so many beautiful church buildings as there are in Europe."

"Two come to mind," Bryce said. "The Basilica of the Holy Blood is on the Burg square. It houses a relic – a vial of blood that supposedly came from Jesus. It's a good idea to get there early to beat the crowd. Then there's Jerusalem Church in a quiet area of the city, but walkable from here. It has an octagonal tower. Inside is a tomb made from black marble, a Gothic stained glass, and a rather spooky chapel containing an effigy of the dead Christ."

After a moment of thought, Bryce added, "Oh yes, another fun, but educational place to visit, is the Choco-Story Museum. It describes chocolate's transition from the cocoa bean into all forms of chocolate. On the way out you go by a room to watch them make chocolate candy and get free samples.

"And, are you ready for this? Another fun stop is the Frites Museum where they tell the story of the humble potato from South America and how it has evolved into a chip. Samples of the frites are fried by a guy who once cooked chips for the Belgian Royal Family."

"Who needs brochures?" Traci laughed.

Later, strolling on their return to the square from seeing the windmills, Traci asked a serious question, catching Bryce by surprise.

"Have you given any thought to the questions I asked regarding your feelings about the creation of the universe and whether you believe there's a Heaven and hell?"

"As a matter of fact I have," Bryce replied. "But I'll admit I haven't dwelled on either topic. When I look around and see the beauty of nature, the moon and stars, the sun, the mountains, the oceans, I'm sure this can't be merely accidental. Some supernatural force has to be making it all come together. You can call me a creationist, but I'm also an evolutionist. I don't find a contradiction between Genesis and Darwin. A bigger piece of the puzzle for me is, if God created everything in the universe, then who – or what – created God?"

"That question has been discussed and debated for centuries," Traci responded. "The answer I like best is there are two types of things in the universe – created things and non-created things – that can exist. All around us we see man-made objects and know, without question, they are created things. Other things, like those found in nature, are also created. The fact these things decay, erode or die over time shows that, left to themselves, they will deteriorate into something less than when they started. Time is even a created thing, because it runs down. So God is an eternal, non-created thing living outside the constraints of time and space. The idea of God not only having an infinite amount of time, but being outside of time altogether, is unique to the Bible. No other religious book makes that claim."

"Uh-huh," Bryce responded. "I have no idea what you just said, but I like the way you said it. Maybe the reason Carl Sagan was an agnostic and Paul Ehrlich an atheist has to do with their not wanting to try to understand what it is you just said."

"Could be," Traci laughed. "Would you like to tackle the Heaven and hell question another time?"

"Yes, please."

CHAPTER EIGHT

THE trip from Bruges, Belgium to Metz, France is an easy five hour train ride through the rural northern France regions of Nord-de-Calais and Champagne-Ardenne before arriving in the Lorraine region, of which Metz is the capital.

Their last day in Bruges had been laid back and enjoyable, having light fun in the Choco-Story and Frites Museums and, for Traci, serious meditation. They decided to get an early start for Metz the next morning. Traci went to her room early to pack and try for a good night's sleep. Bryce, in a pensive mood, feeling somewhat nostalgic, wandered nearby streets where he knew he'd find outdoor cafes and music, ate a cone of frites, had a last Belgium beer and wondered about the wisdom of including Traci in his travel plans.

Both had trouble sleeping.

Traci's mind was grappling with her future. She had never been in limbo before regarding her career. She loved teaching, and while all her experience had been in a parochial setting, she wouldn't be totally opposed to being a public school teacher, or signing on as a faculty member in one of the excellent Marin County private schools. By the time she returned home, it would be late to make application for the fall term. Would it be too late? Should she leave for home now to have more time to find a job? But going back too soon, and without her attorney could screw up their lawsuit strategy. Which was more important? Maybe Bryce would be willing to go back with her and get everything settled quickly.

Tossing on his bed, Bryce's mind was wrapped around the past. This trip – this sentimental journey – placed in the perspective of its goal seemed to be working. The retracing of good times in familiar places brought back warm memories of happiness shared with Lauren. He had been taught as a child in Sunday School when people die and go to Heaven they can look down and see their loved ones and know what they're doing and thinking. Bryce always thought this was more of a scare tactic to keep children on good behavior than based in any religion's theology. But on this night he was hoping it was true, hoping Lauren was seeing and feeling and laughing along with him and wondering what would Lauren think of Traci?

Despite, or maybe due to, the sleeplessness both were earlier than usual in the breakfast room. They quickly ate a small breakfast, checked out of their rooms, had a chatty goodbye conversation with the proprietress – who phoned for a taxi – and headed for the train station, Bryce spurning his usual walk from the hotel to the station.

Hoping not to be asked about her night, Traci suggested Bryce fill her in on Metz and what to expect during their stay. He was eager to comply.

"We had no idea what to expect from Metz, but it's underrated as a destination. We were immediately taken with its architecture and flowers. A stroll through the city can feel like a walk through the centuries."

Bryce continued to explain that in ancient times Metz was known as Divodurum, and was the capital of the Celtic Mediomatrici. At the beginning of the Christian era it was already occupied by the Romans. As the junction of several military roads, and a well-fortified town, it soon became of great importance. One of the last strongholds to surrender to the Germans, it survived the attacks of the Huns before passing, through peaceful negotiations near the end of the 5th century, into the hands of the Franks.

Metz was quite an attraction to royalty. There are numerous reminders of the Roman era which established the city as one of the major centers of the Empire. Remains are evident in a number of the city's museums and, most prominently, in places like Saint-Pierre-aux-Nonnains Basilica, the oldest church in France, dating back to the 4th century. Later, as the cradle of the Carolingian dynasty, Metz became an artistic and cultural Mecca in Europe. In 843 Metz became the capital of the Kingdom of Lorraine and several councils were held there. Numerous books of Holy Writ, the product of the Metz schools of writing and painting, such as the famous Trier Ada manuscript and the Sacramentary of Drogo – now in Paris – are evidence of the active intellectual lives that were led.

The reputation of its schools and craftsmen, the numerous buildings constructed for both religious and secular purposes are outstanding. A magnificent example of 12th century architecture is seen in St. Stephen's Cathedral, one of the tallest in France and resplendent with its use of stained glass windows. Another event that changed the city's destiny was the Franco-Prussian War of 1870. Annexed to Germany by the Treaty of Frankfurt in 1871, a new architectural period began with many large urban building schemes, most obviously seen in the railway station, the central post office and the wide, spacious avenues lined with imposing buildings and townhouses in the German tradition.

Following the armistice with Germany ending the First World War, the French army entered Metz in November 1918 and the city was returned to France at the Treaty of Versailles in 1919. Metz was again annexed by Nazi Germany between 1940 and 1944 during the Second World War, but reverted to France when the war ended.

Lauren had written pages in her journal regarding Metz, and summarized:

In Metz, I felt we were surrounded by the annals of time. I saw Roman chariots racing through the streets, the drivers wearing togas, and laughing children playing with frisky dogs. In the churches I felt the presence of Popes and princes mingling with peasants and paupers. There is wondrous simplicity incased alongside magnificent complexity in the works of art that are found in profusion. In short, Metz is a microcosm of Europe's history, religion, diversity and culture. I love this place!

It was mid-afternoon when the train pulled into Metz. Bryce suggested Traci make herself comfortable in the station's café and guard the luggage while he searched for a hotel. Traci motioned toward the tourist information office as though suggesting maybe that would be a good place to start. He smiled. "That's the avenue of last resort," he said cheerfully. "The avenue of first resort is just outside those doors."

Bryce waved goodbye with fluttering fingers. "I have a place in mind. It's only a block away; if they can't accommodate us, I'll come right back."

The two-star Hotel Bristol held a special place in Bryce's heart. It was here he and Lauren spent their tenth wedding anniversary and was high on their list of places to return someday. Heading south from the station and walking along Rue Lafayette, Bryce was again feeling nostalgic and sad. But – to his surprise – the emotions were not as overwhelming as he thought they would be.

Returning to the station, Bryce was pleased to tell Traci his mission was successfully accomplished and they were registered in rooms on the same floor. After briefly settling in and getting re-freshed, they made their way onto the street for a walking tour of what are, in effect, two towns: the original French quarters, gath-ered around the cathedral, and the Ville allemande, undertaken as a part of a once-and-for-all process of Germanification after King William I of Prussia defeated Napoleon III in 1871. This en-tire quarter was designed to be a model of superior town planning.

Within a few minutes they were at the place de la République, bounded on the east side by shops and cafés and the formal gar-dens of the Esplanade, overlooking the Moselle River, to the west. To the right, as they looked down the esplanade from the square they saw the handsome classical Palais de Justice built with the city's characteristic yellow sandstone. To the left they followed a gravel drive past the old arsenal, now a converted concert hall. They continued on, stopped for a few minutes to look inside the octagonal-shaped 13th century Chapelle des Templiers.

From the north side of place de la Republique, rue des Clercs cuts through the attractive, bustling and largely pedestrianized heart of the old city where most of the shops are found. A short way onto place St-Jacques, Bryce suggested they stop at one of the many outdoor cafés for a drink. Traci suggested a pitcher of beer.

After some small talk Traci sighed deeply.

"Bryce, I'm so grateful to you for suggesting I be a part of this adventure. Everywhere we've been, and all we've done, are so special to me. The nearest I ever came to seeing more of the world was in college when I could have enrolled in a 'semester abroad' enrichment course but turned it down because I wanted to gradu-ate quickly and start my career. Even if I had taken the course, it would have been nothing to match this."

"I'm glad you're here, and happy you feel it's worthwhile," Bryce replied. "It's hard to know what I might have decided by now if you weren't along for the ride. Back in London, and especially when I went out to Bath, I was ready to flick it in. I couldn't concentrate on, or think about anything, or anyone, but Lauren. The one part my therapist didn't prepare me for was how lonely the trip would be. You help fill the void."

"I appreciate knowing that," Traci said. "Sometimes I feel like I'm in the way, that I'm a distraction from your goal."

"Not for a minute, Lady. Not for one minute. Let's be a bit more touristy before we go back. We'll get the outside lay of the land today and spend tomorrow looking inside."

Just a short distance from their refreshment stop is the lofty 12th century Gothic Cathedral of St. Stephens towering above the pedimented and colonnaded classical façade of the Hotel de Ville, the U.S. equivalent to City Hall. The Cathedral boasts the third tallest nave in France; however, its best feature is, without question, the stained glass – both medieval and modern – including windows by Marc Chagall.

From the Cathedral, they took a short walk up rue de Jardins to the city's main museum complex, the Musees de la Cour d'Or, a treasure house of Gallo-Roman sculpture, but equally strong from the medieval and Renaissance periods.

Walking down to the river, they admired the city's compelling townscape and the dramatic view of the Cathedral. They crossed a narrow bridge to the tiny Ile de la Comedie, dominated by its classical 18th century square and theater – the oldest in France – and a rather striking Protestant church, the Temple Nine, erected under the German occupation.

Turning east on their return to the hotel along rue En-Fournirue they passed an old but beautiful square, the place St-Louis with its Gothic arcades and wandered up into the Italianate streets. They ended their walking tour by gazing at the Porte des Allemandes – a massive fortified double gate that once barred the eastern entrances to the medieval city.

Their final stop was to order takeout salads, a baguette of French sourdough and a bottle of wine for dinner.

Traci volunteered to serve as hostess for the light dinner. When the table was set and wine poured, she knocked on Bryce's door. Bryce opened the door and asked a curious question.

"Would it be okay if I brought a guest along?"

Before Traci could respond, Bryce entered her room carrying a photo album.

"If you don't mind," Bryce said softly, "I'd like you to meet Lauren."

"That would be wonderful. I've been hoping since London to really get to know her."

While eating dinner, and before the photo documentary was to begin, Bryce talked about the remainder of their stay in Metz. In his personal itinerary, before meeting Traci, he had scheduled Metz for two days before a day-trip to Luxembourg, and one after. Bryce wondered out loud if this was too long to stay in one place. They could cut Metz a day short and spend more time in Prague; or trade Prague for Vienna; or trade Budapest for Vienna; or eliminate Budapest altogether.

Traci made a "time-out" signal with her hands, went to her shoulder bag, retrieved her copy of Bryce's itinerary, and – less than gently – put it on the table in front of him.

"For a bright lawyer," she said sternly, "some things seem difficult for you to grasp. Please tell me what part of our understanding you don't understand. I'll repeat myself, because you need to be reminded. This is your trip. It's not my trip, it's not our trip. It's your trip. For me to think in any other terms makes me very uncomfortable."

"Okay, sorry teacher," Bryce apologized. "Should I go stand in the corner for a while?"

The agreement was renewed. The itinerary would remain unchanged as to location, but there would be flexibility regarding length of stay. Compromise had re-entered Bryce Gibson's life.

Once dinner was finished and wine glasses refilled, the two sat side by side on the sofa with the album on a low table in front of them. Each picture had a story, starting with their formal wedding portrait and ending with the last picture ever taken of Lauren, one in front of the ski lodge in Seefeld before she got on the tram destined for the mountain. Bryce had carefully selected the pictures. Each included Lauren and, as Bryce narrated the scene, it quickly became obvious to Traci they were pictures from places corresponding to Bryce's "sentimental journey."

Traci was taken by Lauren's striking good looks and imagined her having a demeanor that matched her vivacious, athletic appearance. During two hours of looking and sharing, Bryce's emotions ran the full spectrum. Traci was thoroughly engrossed with each anecdotal episode.

The humor brought laughter to both of them; the final picture brought tears. Later, after a last glass of wine, the two said goodnight with an agreement to be ready for breakfast by eight am.

Traci would rap on Bryce's connecting door letting him know when she was ready.

Once in bed, Traci found herself in a melancholy state of mind. The past two hours were fun, but sad. Fun because it was easy to be with Bryce; sad because he was still feeling pain. On the whole, she reasoned, it was good for him to remember all those times, those happy years he'd shared with Lauren. She felt privileged to be introduced to that part of his life.

As she hugged a pillow, thinking of the love Bryce and Lauren had for each other, she began sobbing. What a wonderful, beautiful life they had together. To love, and be loved, so deeply must be as close to Heaven as one can get while still on earth. Could she have had all this if she hadn't been so cruelly deceived in Philadelphia? Could she have been loved as Lauren was – and still is – loved?

What might be different in her life if the feeling of guilt and the fear of shame hadn't driven her heart into exile? Would she be a successful businesswoman with a loving, doting husband traveling around the world, seeing the elephant and hearing the owl? How many thrilling adventures might she have shared with a husband had she not chosen to spend the prime of her life dressed in simple beige dresses, wearing a wedding ring?

Their first full day in Metz was spent for the most part, as planned, going inside many of the museums and churches they had passed on their walk the afternoon before. For lunch they had quiche Lorraine and then discovered the reason Metz was called the City of Flowers as the two ambled block after block through massive flowerbeds on pathways laid out in serpentine designs.

A mass was being held in St. Stephen's Cathedral and, much to Traci's surprise and delight, Bryce suggested they attend. The organ music was stirring, the choir was inspiring and the homily, while delivered in French, was summarized in both English and German on the printed Order of Worship sheet. When communion was offered, Traci went forward.

Leaving the church after the benediction, Bryce said, "That wasn't too bad at all. The music was great."

"Think you could get used to attending on a regular basis?" Traci asked, smiling as though she knew the answer.

"Could be, who knows? There are a lot of churches in Europe

where I've stood on the outside looking in. The only one I've ever gone through the door more than once is at Notre Dame in Paris. They have great organ concerts."

At the end of the day, they agreed to a quick dinner in the hotel dining room and retired early. Both admitted the night before was restless although neither suggested the reasons. The next morning they would catch an early train for Luxembourg and spend the day exploring its history, culture and monuments. Another day, another adventure.

To be better prepared for the next day's trip, Bryce retrieved Lauren's journal and lay in bed reading her entry for their last trip to Luxembourg.

Up, petit dejeuner in breakfast room next to lobby and out to catch train for Luxembourg. Very cloudy, grey and cold – but we pushed on to see what Luxembourg would hold. Very pretty countryside along the way; wide green fields, well kept villages, deciduous forests and trees in blossom tucked in.

Large train yard was not at all an impressive entry into Luxembourg but on our walk of discovery, when we reached the bridge over a very deep ravine cutting through the middle of the city, it takes on a gracious and festive appearance with a medieval to 17th century look. Part of the reason for the festive ambience, we learned, had to do with the fete today in celebration of the Duke's birthday.

Sun broke out of clouds from time to time, so pictures may (hopefully) capture what would take a lot of words. We were drawn, as is often the case, to an imposing cathedral and found it an unusual mix of Renaissance and Baroque. The best part of this visit was arriving as a photo artist was hanging a moving and very current exhibit of 40 matted and framed photos (about 20 x 24 or so) all around the nave – pictures taken in Rome before and during the days of Pope John Paul II funeral – waiting masses and individuals, including bishops, gendarmes posted for crowd control, pictures of people waiting to see the Pope's body, people in sleeping bags. Amazing stories captured on film by this artist. What a dramatic series, taking on special meaning in the context of the cathedral.

Left the cathedral and walked about in residential areas with grand town houses looking 17th – 18th century, parks, pedestrian malls. Walked along the grand ravine and over a very high bridge to what appeared to be a chateau, but disappointingly for my romantic streak, now houses a bank. Through more narrow streets, along wide boulevards, down a rather steep narrow street lined with narrow houses we'd seen coming through town in our first hour. We followed it to the bottom and found a whole "other" village tucked in at the base of the steep canyon walls.

Slate roofs are all that is seen for roofing, whether on grand homes or humble. Looking down on all angles of rooflines makes for a unity in all the irregularity very picturesque. At about 3:00 the cathedral bells began to ring, and rang continuously for a whole hour, very likely to honor the Duke. A five-hour walkabout and then to the station for return to Metz. Splendid day!

Bryce sighed deeply, closed the journal and kissed the cover, turned out the light and fell fast asleep.

CHAPTER NINE

THE French term for breakfast is petit dejeuner and consists traditionally of a light flaky croissant served with coffee or tea and juice. Almost always when in France, Bryce would leave the room while Lauren was still sleeping, to find a neighborhood boulangerie where the morning bread was still warm. It was his habit to stock up on little individually packaged containers of jam, jelly and honey from bed and breakfast dining areas to have available in the room, as needed for a quick morning start.

When Traci knocked to let Bryce know she was ready to face the day, he opened the door and invited her in. The aroma of warm croissants and fresh coffee brewing in the carafe provided by the hotel greeted Traci. The table was simply set with cocktail napkins for plates, each with a croissant, plastic knives, pats of butter and little tubs of toppings in a plastic glass matching the ones containing orange juice. Packets of sugar and non-dairy creamers of various flavors were next to the coffee carafe. The coffee cups were made of heavy heat-resistant paper with fold out handles.

"Bonjour, mademoiselle," Bryce said in a heavy French accent. "A table for one?"

"No, a table for two," Traci replied with a broad smile. "I'm expecting a kooky friend to arrive at any minute."

An hour later, on the train to Luxembourg, Traci was still amused by Bryce's surprise petit dejeuner, her first French breakfast. She was learning something more about him every day. Underneath his exterior of quiet demeanor, a real man stood in the shadows patiently waiting to step into the sunlight at any appropriate moment. Traci was beginning to suspect Bryce's nerdish persona was more by design than anything based in reality.

As the train pulled out of Thionville, one of only two stops between Metz and Luxembourg City, Traci said, "I've started a new hobby. I'm now a collector of countries. So far in my box I have England, France and Belgium. Will I be able to add Luxembourg?

Is it a stand-alone country or a part of another? Both Luxembourg and Liechtenstein have just been names to me. I was never big on geography until now."

"Both Luxembourg and Liechtenstein are sovereign countries. Luxembourg is much larger and has had a more prominent role in the shaping of Europe. Look on your Eurail map and you'll find Liechtenstein wedged between Austria and Switzerland on the route from Innsbruck and Zurich. Luxembourg is ruled by a duke; therefore the country is referred to as the Grand Duchy of Luxembourg. Liechtenstein's ruler of its 35,000 inhabitants is a prince, so it's called a Principality."

Traci once again became a student listening to Bryce's orientation to Luxembourg.

"Over a thousand years ago, in late 900's Count Siegfried, who was a descendent of Charlemagne, was given deed to a rocky promontory overlooking the Alzette River valley where a small stronghold had been situated, probably constructed by the Romans, and the name Luxembourg first appeared in history. That name would pass to the city that grew up around the fortress, and then be handed on to the name of the country which developed around the city. Today, the city and country carry the same name."

Traci was intrigued as Bryce continued, explaining that Siegfried expanded the small stronghold into a veritable fortress and the city of Luxembourg remained a fortress city for almost a thousand years before it was dismantled in 1867. The city's population was never large in numbers, with 5,000 at the beginning of the 14th century; 8,500 by the end of the 18th century; and 45,000 immediately after the First World War. Today there are about 100,000 people who call Luxembourg home.

From the time the fortress was built until its demise it was home to knights and soldiers who were billeted there in large numbers. Artisans and traders settled all around, first on top of the rocky outcrop and others spilling out beneath it. This created a distinction between the upper and lower city.

Certain cities owe their origins to a religious sanctuary, to an abbey, to the passage of a river, or a crossing of the ways. Luxembourg owes its heritage to its precipitous location and the military interest it attracted. An example of its strategic importance was seen during the 19th century during the conflict between the Bourbons and the Hapsburgs with Luxembourg at the very front line between France and Germany.

Thanks to the Treaty of London, the Grand Duchy was declared a neutral state. Although the treaty called for the fortifications to be dismantled, there are still remains of the impressive ramparts.

Leaving the train and checking on the return schedule to Metz, Bryce suggested, because of the shortness of time, the best and most efficient way to tour the city was to follow the "Wenzel Walk" which guides visitors through 1000 years of history in 100 minutes. The name pays tribute to Wenceslas II, Duke of Luxembourg from 1383 to 1419.

This cultural and historical self-guided tour is a walk through the oldest quarters of the city and passes by many architecturally compelling edifices. A large array of information boards posted along the way supply details of the most important sights and history.

The promenade starts on the Bock Promontory, the cradle of the city, from where the walkers have a magnificent panorama of the Alzette valley. Below the street are archeological crypts and casements hewn into the rock.

Further along is Castle Bridge, built from red sandstone in 1735. Crossing the bridge, the walk continues along the so-called Corniche, set up by the Spaniards in the 17th century and fortified by Vauban later on. It is lined by some remarkable houses, noble dwellings from the 17th, 18th and 19th centuries and a picturesque terraced row of houses with shops and restaurants. Continuing down, there is the bastioned Grund Gate, also built by the Spaniards in 1632. Turning left and meandering further down the hill there is a small footbridge called Steichen. Towers rising above and in front play epoch musical pieces. This part of the city wall functioned as defense for the inhabitants of the valley. It linked the so-called Upper Town and the Rham Plateau, with its higher location, into the defense ring of the city.

The Moat in front of the wall was uncovered by archeologists in 1992. Among other things, they disclosed the very-well kept foundation of a medieval wooden bridge, which was part of the first highway to Trier. Also, two exterior moat walls were uncovered, one medieval and the other one dating back to the Spanish domination.

Crossing the sentry walk of the battlements fitted out with loopholes, the tour leads past the Tutesall, which is part of a complex of buildings forming the Neumunster Abbey. After the first abbey was destroyed, the Benedictine monks settled in what was then St. John's Hospital in 1547 and built several new buildings. In 1796 the monks were driven out in the aftermath of the French

Revolution and the cloister over the years served as a prison, a military hospital and finally, after extensive renovation, it has become a major venue for social and cultural events.

Ascending a staircase from the abbey, the walk passes the Second Gate of Trier built in 1590. A bridge leads across the road to the Rham Plateau. Following the outer walls of the former barracks and leaving the plateau by a staircase leading back into the valley, walkers bump into the Blesserpuert which also dates to the 15th century. In 1907 the front part of this old city gate was demolished, only to be restored again in the 1980s.

The promenade then progresses through St. Ulric Street until, on the right-hand side, a small path leads to the bank of the Alzette where parts of the Grund Lock, built in 1731, can be seen. After a short walk along the river bank an elevator is waiting to take passengers to the Holy Ghost Plateau on which, in the 13th century, a cloister was built for use by the order of St. Clare nuns. In 1684 French Marshal Vauban used the available space to build a citadel and two barracks, both of which were in use until 1967.

The Wetzel Walk concludes at this point.

"I have to get memory cards that hold more pictures," Traci complained on their way back to the train station. "I took more than a hundred pictures over the past two hours."

"Isn't there a way to delete the ones you don't want?" Bryce asked.

"Yes, but I want them all. I went through my Metz pictures last night and didn't dump one of them. Everything is so beautiful. I want to remember it all."

Within 15 minutes of the train departing Luxembourg for Metz, Traci suggested she needed a power nap to replace energy lost on the Wetzel Walk. Since she and Bryce were the only two in their six-passenger compartment, Bryce suggested she stretch out on one of the bench seats constructed for three people. He offered his rucksack for a pillow and within a very short while she was asleep.

Bryce sat looking at her sleeping form and was again impressed with her beauty. And, that aside, he was becoming very impressed with her as a strong, independent woman. He had long since stopped trying to figure her out; wondering what thoughts were running through her head; what all has happened to make her who she is. The lawyer in him wanted to ask dozens of questions, the human spirit in him, the "gracious sensitivity factor" Lauren called it, kept the lawyer in check.

CHAPTER TEN

THE travel time from Metz to Prague is 13 hours with one train change in Nuremberg, Germany and another in the Czech Republic border town of Cheb. After returning to Metz from Luxembourg and having dinner in a small, but upscale, Italian restaurant near the hotel, Bryce suggested they leave Metz in the early evening the next day and spend the night on the train. This would assure their arrival in Prague by mid-afternoon.

The first time Bryce and Lauren tried getting from Cheb to Prague turned into a frustrating fiasco. They had spent a few days in the beautiful town of Bayreuth, Germany, having discovered they were celebrating their annual "Spring Asparagus Festival." Lauren loved asparagus in every way fashion and form, so not making the Bayreuth stop was non-negotiable.

In order to make the journey from Bayreuth to Prague as seamless as possible, Bryce suggested they go to Cheb a day early. Eurail passes were not honored in the Czech Republic so they needed to purchase a point-to-point ticket from Cheb to Prague. They also had been told reservations were required.

Lauren's journal reflected the situation.

In Bayreuth we boarded a small two-car train serving the commuter needs of passengers going to and from Cheb. Arriving in Cheb we discovered a rather drab station. No marketing of any goods and no passenger seating. Ticket windows and schedule displays were all we saw; but that was all we needed.

When we inquired about tickets, we found out very quickly that communication would be a challenge and I would need to keep my phrase book (which I had left in our hotel room) at the ready. Bryce showed the ticket agent our written itinerary – which was accepted and understood – showing the time we wanted tickets and reservations to Prague. The agent wrote the price of 308 Koruna on a slip of paper. When Bryce offered a credit card for payment, non-verbal (and something in a stream of verbal) reactions clearly indicated credit cards were not accepted.

The agent pointed to a currency exchange across the way, so off we went. Fortunately, an exchange-rate was posted beside the window giving the current rate of exchange for buying Euros, so we got enough (and considerably more than enough) Koruna to pay for the tickets and reservations. Now, owning a pot full of money, we got the tickets which were recorded on a single slip of paper. When Bryce carefully studied the tickets (as he always does) he noted the date for travel was today! Yikes! I hadn't indicated which date we wanted to travel.

So, with a face looking as apologetic as I could conger, along with a calendar, I approached the woman behind the counter. Even before I reached the window, she had thrown her hands in the air and was saying loudly "Yi Yi Yi" for all to hear. Finally, we were on the same track (pun intended) and we had new tickets for the right day! Double Yikes!

Before checking out of the Hotel Bristol, Bryce requested the manager go online to see if rooms were available at the Beetle Pension in Prague and, if so, to reserve two. Bryce had discovered there is a rapport between hotel management that is more productive in getting reservations than individual travelers. Within 20 minutes, confirmed reservations were received for the next day.

Traci, with her trademark smile, feigned disappointment. "Darn, does this mean I don't get to play bag-guard while you traipse around looking for lodging?"

———————

The overnight trip on through Germany was pleasant enough, with a short a stop in Heidelberg where they got off long enough for Traci to take pictures of the castle. Fortunately, they had the six-passenger seating compartment to themselves so they could stretch out. Both slept through the whistle-stop at Warzburg and Bryce was only dozing lightly when they reached Nuremberg.

Before waking Traci from a deep sleep for the train change, Bryce again looked at his traveling companion. In so many ways, Traci and Lauren were similar. Both were strong willed and intelligent; both were attractive without ever flaunting the fact; both were easy to be with. They would have been great friends had they known each other.

Bryce gently nudged Traci's shoulder to wake her. She stirred slightly. He tried again, this time with some verbal encouragement.

"Come on, Lauren, we have to change trains."

They both recognized his faux pas at the same time and he tried quickly to remedy the situation.

"Oh gosh, Traci, I'm sorry."

"Please don't be," Traci replied, rubbing the sleep from her eyes. "You just gave me a wonderful compliment."

"I was thinking before I woke you how much you and Lauren are alike."

"That's nice to know, Bryce, it really is" Traci said. She was quiet for sometime before adding, "But keep in mind, while I may be like Lauren, I'm not her. Fair enough?"

"More than fair enough," Bryce responded.

The layover in Nuremburg was almost two hours, just enough time to stretch their legs and have a taste of some authentic German cuisine. Since Traci was going to add Germany to her country collection, she suggested they go out into the city and walk around the block. It was a brilliant, star filled night. Floodlights bathed the magnificent twin spires of the 262 feet tall St. Lorenz Cathedral in warm amber light. Even at this very late hour, shops and restaurants were bustling with customers.

They found a nearby open-air beer garden, ordered wiener schnitzel and zinfandel wine while watching people, mostly couples, stroll down the broad avenue. Traci, reaching for Bryce's hand, discovered his hand moving toward hers. Their hands met, their fingers entwined, their eyes danced.

Before boarding the train for Cheb, Bryce summarized Lauren's journal account of the Cheb encounter. They found a currency exchange in the Nuremburg station and each traded Euros for a fistful of Koruna. Eagle Scout Gibson was now prepared.

————————

Having learned from the remembered experience, the ticket and reservation purchase in Cheb went smoothly and within an hour of their arrival from Nuremburg were on their way to Prague.

"What should I know about the Czech Republic, Professor Gibson?" Traci asked.

"There's a wealth of history here," Bryce replied. "Gliding along on the train through this spectacular rural countryside, it's difficult to imagine the centuries of war, upheaval, rebellion, murder and mayhem interwoven into the country's fabric since its founding in the year 870. Situated in the heart of Europe, the problems confronting the Czech people were never contained to being just local. They have been invaded by the Hapsburgs, the Nazis and the Soviets.

"The Hussite Wars were the result of the country's 1418 rejection of Roman Catholicism; the revolt of 1618 against Hapsburg rule set in motion the tumultuous Thirty Year's War; the German annexation of Sudetenland – a region of Germany given to the Czechs after WWI – in 1938 was a major event leading to WWII.

"Before and during World War I, the Czechs and Slovaks were separate sovereign republics. Eventually, under pressure from the United States and other European nations the Czechs and Slovaks, on October 28, 1918, signed an agreement forming the Czechoslovak Republic. Prague was designated the capital. Everything remained relatively stable but in 1946 the Communists became the largest party and formed a coalition which led, in 1948, to a coup d'état with the backing of the Soviet Union.

"In the 1960s, with most of the world living in moderately peaceful environments, the Czechoslovak Communist Party initiated reforms designed to lead the country toward democracy. The result was the invasion of Prague on August 20, 1968 by more than 200,000 Soviet and Warsaw Pact troops. An iron-fist government controlled the country until Soviet Premier Gorbachev embraced perestroika and glasnost which led to the eventual dismantling of the Soviet Union. On January 1, 1993 Czechoslovakia split into the Czech and Slovak Republics. The Czech Republic joined NATO in 1999 and in a 2003 referendum voted to join the European Union in 2004."

"Your knowledge of history is amazing," Traci said with sincerity.

"It's something I've always loved," Bryce replied. "While most other kids were reading comic books, I was in the library reading history books."

———————

The Beetle Pension is situated in one of the central quarters of Prague and easily reachable from the train station by tram, bus or subway. On nice days it's an easy half-hour walk from the historic center of Prague to the Beetle.

As Bryce and Traci waited at the tram stop near the train station, Traci asked, "What's the difference between a pension and a hotel?"

"That's a good question," Bryce replied, "and one I didn't have an answer to until our first trip. Most hotels are in large buildings, many of them constructed for the purpose of providing lodging. In Europe, they may or may not include breakfast in the daily rate, as opposed to the traditional B & B, where breakfast is always a part of the deal.

"Pensions are, almost exclusively, renovated space from small townhouses or flats. While the rooms in a pension can have as much ambience as a nice hotel, many of them have only one bathroom on each floor, shared by all. Not to worry, though, at the Beetle all nine apartments come with their own bathrooms."

The trams in Prague, while reminiscent of the San Francisco trolleys, are longer and narrower and make fewer stops. The walk from the tram stop to the Beetle covered six blocks, the last two down a sloping, tree lined residential street. If it weren't for the sign reading "Accommodations" above the entry door, the pension would be indiscernible among the row houses running on both sides of the street.

A push on the doorbell button brought an immediate response through the intercom and after Bryce identified himself, they were buzzed in and greeted by their host, a young man with a good command of English.

"Will your friends be coming along shortly?" he asked.

"No, it's just the two of us," Bryce answered.

"I'm sorry," the young man said. "We have recorded you requested two rooms."

"Yes, that's right. We'll need two rooms, one for each of us."

"So sorry," the young man apologized. "I thought. . ."

"It's okay," Bryce said with a chuckle. "We get a lot of that."

As they were taking their bags to their rooms, Bryce noticed a new customer service feature had been added in a small room off the lobby. There, on a large wooden table was a computer, complete with internet connectivity, a color printer and a combined scanner/fax. A note requested residents obtain an access code from the desk clerk.

"It's probably a good idea to check for email messages while we're here," Bryce suggested. "I've lost track of days, but it seems quite a while since I looked to see what might be going on at the office."

"Good idea," Traci concurred. "I'm a little less upset with Michael than I was. I'll send him a note to let him know I'm safe."

"Let's get settled, do a neighborhood walkabout, grab a bite to eat and then enter the world of cyberspace," Bryce suggested. "We need to get an early start tomorrow. This is a fabulous city with much more to see than we'll be able to cover while we're here. Tonight I'll make a list of "must-dos" and we can attack it right after breakfast in the morning. You'll definitely need to add to your supply of memory cards. Prague's a non-stop photo op."

It was later than they had hoped when they returned. The walkabout was intriguing and Traci didn't want it to end. She was mesmerized by the music everywhere, with the city's love affair with jazz and blues. They ate at a sidewalk café where the menu entrees were displayed in color photographs. Traci pointed to one containing chicken; Bryce selected a pork and rice casserole.

Back at the pension, Bryce found the desk clerk in the breakfast room drinking coffee and got the internet access code. He suggested Traci do her emailing first and get to bed while he went to his room to start making a list on the next day's sightseeing schedule. The old tried-and-true rapping on his door when she finished with the computer was to be the signal.

When the rap came, Bryce said goodnight through the door. When another rap sounded, he went to the door and found Traci holding sheets of paper.

"Here are my emails," she said with an edge of anger in her voice. "You need to read these."

The first one was from Bishop Grogan, sent the day after her letter to him from London. Bryce carefully read the message.

Sister Teresa:

I'm astonished at such blatant disrespect for me, for your colleagues, and for the Church! Your threat of legal action has fallen on deaf ears. Why would you even think of dragging the Church through such an ugly ordeal?

Have you no appreciation for the way the Church has cared for you, looked after you, accepted you into one of its most revered orders, allowed you to teach our children, and provided a place for you to live? Shame on you!

Now you're hiding out someplace in the world rather than step-

ping forward to admit your wrong-doing and seek forgiveness, not only from God, but also from the man you tried to destroy by lusting after him. How many other innocent souls will you hurt if you follow through with your self-centered plan to bring suit?

Excommunication is not a pleasant proceeding. Let me remind you: if you cause by word, deed or example an act that spreads division and confusion among the Faithful, it is necessary for the Church to clarify the situation by means of a formal announcement informing the laity you are not a person to follow, and the clergy that you, by your own willful acts, have separated yourself from the Church and you are no longer to receive the sacraments.

It is my sincere prayer you will choose not to have such an embarrassing circumstance befall you.

Yours in Christ,

Bishop Robert Grogan, S. J.

The second email, sent a week later, was from a lawyer whose firm represented Bishop Grogan and the diocese.

Dear Sister Teresa:

Allow me to introduce myself. My name is Zachary Tillson. I'm with the San Francisco law firm of Grassley, Leklem, Olson & Marrs. We represent Bishop Robert Grogan and the diocese he leads. Bishop Grogan has informed us of your potential future legal action against the Bishop and the Church. While this would be unfortunate, it is perfectly within your discretion to do so.

However, before acting too hastily, I would appreciate the opportunity to meet with your attorney to consider the possibility of working out some compromise by which we can avoid going to trial, thus sparing you a great deal of time and expense. While the Bishop is adamant, at this point, he would be against any agreement wherein either he or the Church would assume culpability in this matter, I'm confident he can be convinced otherwise.

I understand you are out of the county for an extended stay. It will not be necessary for you to be present if/when there is a conference. I look forward to hearing from your attorney in the near future.

Very sincerely yours,

Zachary Tillson

The third email was from her brother, Michael, and had been sent recently.

Cait –

Pardon my French, but WHAT THE DEVIL IS GOING ON? I've received both an email letter and a phone call from your Bishop Grogan insisting I try to put some sense into your head. What's this stuff about you suing the Bishop and his diocese?

I know how angry you are, I saw that hit the fan when you stormed out of here. But what are you trying to prove with a law suit? It'll be another black eye for the Church. We're finally getting back on track after all these pedophile claims, and now you come along stirring the pot with a different spoon.

There was a time when you always put others first. There was never a selfish act or a self-centered thought in your head. Why now, all the sudden, do you find it necessary to call attention to yourself in such a destructive way?

Can't you just let it go, if not for yourself, then for me? You know I'm in line to be named Auxiliary Bishop of the Trenton diocese. The reason for Grogan's phone call was to drop a not-too-subtle hint that if you don't back away from your threat to sue, he'll work hard to screw up my appointment.

I thought I would never have to call in the marker I've held all these years; but it looks like this is the time. You owe me, Cait.

Michael

Bryce placed the printouts of the three emails side by side.

"Well, for sure, we have the Bishop's attention. What we see here is a classic 'bad cop-good cop' scenario. Grogan comes on strong with threats; Tillson counters with a way out. Then for good measure, they throw in sibling pressure. I know Zach Tillson, we partner up in a charity golf tournament every spring, and I run into him occasionally at the court house. He's a good lawyer and a good man."

"And, for sure, the Bishop has my attention," Traci said. "But I'm more concerned with hindering Michael's advancement opportunity than the possibility of being excommunicated. I'm not even sure I want to stay in the Church; certainly not in any official capacity."

"But what happens if you're excommunicated?"

"Excommunication doesn't have the stigma it once did. Basically, if I'm excommunicated I'll be barred from teaching in a Catholic school and from receiving the Eucharist or other sacraments. I can still attend Mass. I've been pretty much setting my own rules for the past few years anyway. I hadn't gone to confession for more than a year until I went the evening I stayed behind at Our Lady's in Bruges. That, in itself, is grounds for excommunication. If I'm officially excommunicated and want to take communion or go to confession, I will; with the exception of my home parish."

"So, we can call the Bishop's bluff?" Bryce asked.

"Absolutely. But it'll be great if we can get Michael out of harm's way. It's Clifton Norton's hide I want to nail to the wall."

"And we will," Bryce said. "Let's sleep on it. We may need to tweak our strategy a bit. I'm curious about Michael's last statement in his email. What kind of marker are you holding that he'll call in?"

"I'll sleep on that too. Let's talk in the morning."

It was another restless night for both. Bryce focused on draft responses to Grogan and Tillson; Traci wrestled with the best way to explain Michael's comment.

At breakfast, Bryce shared his hand-written response to Grogan for Traci's review and suggestions.

Bishop Grogan:

I have received your reprimand and your threat of my excommunication. My first reaction was to reply using the same angry tone you set in your letter to me. But after a great deal of prayer and supplication in asking the Lord for guidance, He led my heart and soul to a quiet place; I am now at peace.

It was never my desire to bring harm to the Church. As I told you in my first letter, my faith in my God and my Church is unfaltering. I am forever in its debt. Also, it was never my desire to bring harm to you or your staff at the school. On the other hand, I have been considerably harmed.

I don't believe this was a deliberate or malicious act on your part but rather a consequence of snap-judgment. Had you taken more time and provided me a fair hearing, perhaps things would not have escalated to this level of animosity.

As you are aware, I have also received a letter from your attorney, Mr. Tillson, requesting a meeting with my attorney to discuss a possible settlement of this matter without going to court. I am providing a copy of that letter to my attorney for his response.

Sincerely,

Treasa Dunne

"You do have a way of expressing what I'm feeling," Traci said. "I wouldn't change a word."

"Thank you," Bryce said, handing her another sheet of yellow legal pad paper. "Here's what I propose to send to Tillson."

Dear Zach –

Disney was right, it is a small world!

My client, Sister Treasa Dunne, has forwarded your letter with instructions for me to contact you, as you requested. Sister Treasa is out of the country for an undetermined time seeking solace for the pain and humiliation inflicted upon her by your client, Bishop Robert Grogan.

While I am willing to meet with you at some convenient time in the future, that cannot occur until Sister Treasa returns to the U.S. and she and I have the opportunity to discuss the case in detail. We will also need time to assess the damage to her reputation which, undoubtedly, has resulted from gossip and innuendo.

On a related matter, Sister Treasa informs me your client has contacted her brother, Father Michael Dunne, now on assignment in Ireland. Father Michael is one step from being appointed to the position of Coadjutor Bishop of the Trenton, New Jersey diocese. Please inform your client of the consequences of an unsolicited negative recommendation. Should he do or say anything that would interfere with Father Michael's receiving this appointment, all chances of a negotiated settlement will be off the table.

I, too, am out of the City for a lengthy period of time attending to personal matters relating to the untimely death of my wife, Lauren. As soon as I'm back, I'll give you a call.

With best regards,

Bryce Gibson

"That's perfect," Traci commented. "I really like the way your mind works."

"Let's get these sent right away," Bryce said. "You need to decide how to reply to Michael. I know you'll want to make it personal, so I don't need be a part of that."

It was a beautiful, sunshiny day. Bryce had worked a schedule designed to give an overview of Prague. Working with a map of the city, he had identified places of interest and the best route for walking. Before beginning the trek, Bryce again asked Traci if she cared to explain Michael's remark about the marker.

"It's something very hurtful that happened a long time ago," Traci replied. "I can't imagine it will have any bearing on our case."

"You'll need to trust me to decide if it will or not. That's why you're paying me the big bucks. When we pull Norton into this, he'll have his goons swarming everywhere digging for dirt. I don't want to be blindsided."

"It's not dirt, really; just a very traumatic time in my life." They sat on a bench in front of the pension as Traci began explaining Michael's remark. "What I'm going to tell you has never been discussed with anyone – except Michael."

"Traci, before you start, do you understand what's meant by 'attorney-client privilege'? As your attorney, I'm bound by law and the ethics of my profession to keep everything you confide in me totally safeguarded."

"Yes, I understand; but thanks for reassuring me."

"I can tell this won't be easy for you. You can tell me now or later," Bryce said, squeezing her hand gently. "Take all the time you need." She thought for a long minute, and then related her story.

When she started college, Traci declared English Literature as her major field of interest; but ended up graduating with a degree in business and marketing. Her father had always planned for Michael to take over the Guinness distributorship when he retired. When Michael felt the call to the priesthood, her father couldn't have been happier. She remembered the day clearly when he came to her and asked, "Treasa Roisin, my pet, how would you like to be a businesswoman?" She was thrilled by the idea. Within a week after graduating from Immaculata, she was in the office learning the ropes. The activity was fast-paced and the environment was electric. The first assignment she got from her father was to create a television commercial pitting Guinness against Budweiser. It knocked his socks off.

She was on top of the world. Then things got even better. For years her father had cooperated with the University of Pennsylvania's Wharton Business School by providing an internship opportunity each term for one of their graduate students. That year it was Kevin Sampson, and he was beautiful. Although he was older and more experienced in business than Traci, she was assigned to be his mentor and supervisor. He proved to be extremely talented. They spent every possible minute together, working to develop TV and radio spots, display ads for newspapers, and designing billboards. He was on a leave of absence from his firm in New York City and traveled there on weekends to stay involved.

She was swept off her feet, falling head over heels in love. He was living in a loft apartment near the Penn campus while Traci had settled into a small two-bedroom condo near city center. Since the office was located within walking distance of her place, they spent more and more time there after work. A couple of nights a week he would sleep over.

Kevin was Jewish. Traci couldn't have cared less, but they decided to keep the affair secret until she felt her parents would accept her being in love with a non-Catholic. Traci's mother had been planning a big church wedding since Traci was ten years old. Kevin's internship was the last requirement for his graduate degree. He had done a great job and Traci was able to write a glowing recommendation for his file. To celebrate, they went to Cape May on the Jersey shore. This was their first weekend together and it was to be a glorious time. Traci made reservations at the luxurious Washington Inn, renovated from an 1840s plantation house. Everything was first class: their room was beautiful and the restaurant glowed with candlelit romance. Traci had spent hours in Strawbridge's and Macy's shopping for just the right dress and negligee. She wanted everything to be perfect.

She had known for a week she was pregnant, but decided not to share the good news until they were in Cape May. She was happy with the thought of making a baby with Kevin. They had an intimate dinner and danced until after midnight. Before leaving the restaurant for their room, she poured each a glass of champagne and proposed a toast. Standing by the table, with their glasses raised, she said, "Here's to our baby and our beautiful future together." Kevin's face turned white and his hands shook. He sat down quickly; the glass fell to the floor.

Then, with three words, her life began to unravel. "Traci, I'm married."

"What a terrible thing to hear, even if you weren't pregnant," Bryce said. "The guy's a real jerk."

"Yes, he is. The second the blood drained from his face I knew I'd been used. I felt so devastated, so vulnerable. I was totally naïve. Then I began feeling unclean, inside and out. We went back to the room and I lost it. I yelled obscenities I had no idea I even knew. I threw his clothes and suitcase into the hallway and locked the door. The next morning he was gone. Since we had driven down in my car, I don't know where he spent the night, or how he got out of Cape May. He simply disappeared."

"Didn't you have any way to reach him in New York?" Bryce asked.

"I'm sure I could have found him if I'd wanted to. But why go looking for the snake that just bit you? From that night until today, I've had no contact with him.

"When I got to Philadelphia Saturday night, I was in such a state of depression I tried to commit suicide. I got stinko drunk, took a handful of Excedrin PM, wrote Kevin a pathetic goodbye note and lay down on my bed to die. I woke up at noon on Sunday, disoriented and confused. I went into the bathroom to throw up and found an empty multi-vitamin bottle on the floor."

Bryce bit his lower lip to stifle a laugh.

Traci called Michael and he came right over. He had just been ordained and was assigned as an associate pastor of the parish church where they grew up. He loved his job. When he got to her place she was a mess; her condo was a mess; her life was a mess.

"I didn't have to say a word when he arrived. He looked around the room, and then looked at me. He took me in his arms and said 'I love you baby sister. Whatever it is, I love you.' I knew then it would be all right; I could talk to him as a brother – as a priest – and he would help me sort it out. I told him of my misguided love for Kevin and the attempt to take my life, but not the pregnancy."

"Traci, as your attorney I don't need to know anything more," Bryce said. "There's nothing here Norton can use against you."

"But I'd like to tell you the rest, as a friend," Traci responded. "If I'm making you uncomfortable, I'll stop."

"It's your comfort you need to consider, not mine," Bryce said. "It's not important for me to know, but if it's important for you to share, please do."

Tears were beginning to glisten in Traci's eyes. She reached into her shoulder bag and found a packet of tissues as she began to reveal the most excruciating, most tormented time of her life.

For eight days after she split with Kevin, she had gone through purgatory, into hell, and back to Earth again looking for answers to the agonizing questions blocking her doorway to sleep. She thought of her parents and the faith they had in her; of their unquestioning trust she would always do right. She wanted to run away.

A lifetime of religious dogma permeated every conscious consideration. Finally, the crucible being waged in her tortured soul reached a verdict: abortion.

Under the Code of Canon Law, a Catholic woman who has an abortion is automatically excommunicated by the law itself if the abortion is directly intended, is successful, and if the woman involved knew the penalty of excommunication was attached to the law forbidding abortion. Traci, aware of the consequences of her act, nonetheless chose to abort the fetus. She wanted a baby – but not his baby. The child would be a constant reminder of her foolish, albeit unintended, mistake.

A few days after the procedure, Traci contacted Michael and arranged for him to hear her confession. As her brother, he was loving and heartsick; as her priest, he was loving and forgiving. Her secret would be theirs to keep.

Although her full confession and finding peace in the Sacrament of Reconciliation allowed the healing process to begin, Traci was not satisfied those rites alone were sufficient to restore her feelings of self worth and dignity. That could only be accomplished by joining a religious order and committing her life to helping others.

"I immediately quit working for my father and entered a training program leading to confirmation. My life from that point has been focused on serving the church."

"There's a mantra in the legal profession," Bryce said. "The time should fit the crime. You've served your time, and then some."

As they stood to begin their trek, Bryce took this remarkable woman in his arms and held her securely until the tension left her body and she relaxed.

CHAPTER ELEVEN

TREASA Roisin Alana Caitlin Irene Dunne was born into a happy family. Her father, Patrick, was the son of a hard-working Irish immigrant who, through tenacity and grit, moved up the corporate ladder of the Guinness brewing empire to become the company's top executive in the greater Philadelphia region. Her mother, the former Cecilia Colcannon, was raised in Upper Darby Township, a suburb west of Philadelphia. Patrick was the youngest of seven children; Cecilia the youngest of five.

Patrick and Cecilia were both lively, gregarious children who met as teenagers while appearing live on Dick Clark's American Bandstand televised dance program. They were paired as partners for eight consecutive Saturday afternoon shows and twice were asked by the host to rate dance tunes. Although they lived some miles apart and attended different high schools, they dated steadily until they married immediately after Patrick graduated from Drexel University's LeBow School of Business. Patrick's siblings all became homesick for Ireland and moved back, one after another, before Patrick was graduated.

A year later when Cecilia became pregnant with Michael, she quit her job as a floral designer and dedicated the rest of her life to being a mother. Patrick went into the beer distribution business with his father and in five years was made a partner. Six years later Patrick's father, by then a widower, retired and returned to Galway to live out his life. Patrick assumed full ownership of the business. In addition to the distributorship, Patrick was given the deed to his parent's estate near Ardmore on Philadelphia's Main Line.

The Main Line gets its name from the Main Line of the Pennsylvania Railroad constructed in the 19th century. At that time, the Railroad owned much of the land surrounding the tracks and promoted the construction of sprawling estates to attract Philadelphia's elite. The scenery is one of rolling hills, open meadows and winding roads. This, combined with magnificent homes, many of the best public and private schools in the nation, first-class shopping, top-rated restaurants, professional services and unsurpassed recreational facilities makes the Main Line one of the most desirable upscale suburban locations in the country.

While the Dunnes had money, they never flaunted it. For Patrick the home was a quiet retreat at the end of the long workday. Also, it was good for his business to entertain customers and potential customers and to provide a relaxing retreat setting for his staff's planning and marketing strategy sessions. For Cecelia it was a safe haven for her children. For the two children it was a perfect childhood as they rode horses through the woods and bicycles over paved trails to their hearts' content.

It would have been easy for Michael and Traci to feel smug and superior relating to others if their parents had allowed it to happen. To the contrary, Patrick and Cecelia made sure their children became grounded – and remained grounded – in the true meaning of the Golden Rule. As a result, both became involved in organizing youth groups to assist the elderly, feed the hungry, and collect toys for distribution at Christmas. They, and their small army of junior workers, would set fundraising goals for worthy projects and develop strategic plans for meeting those goals. Without fail the goals would always be reached; although on occasion a last-minute anonymous donation would save the day.

Pressure on the children to succeed was never applied and, as a result, they succeeded on their own. They were allowed to make many of their own decisions with the understanding it was their responsibility to follow through. Discussions were held on every important issue. Both Michael and Traci chose where they would like to attend school. Michael selected public school; Traci, two years later, decided on St. Leonard's Academy. Michael attributed his call to the priesthood as having been exposed to the sins of the world. Traci wanted an academic challenge. Both were satisfied with their decisions, for the most part.

However, there were times in retrospect when Traci questioned the wisdom of her choices. Was an all-female learning environment the best thing? If she had enrolled in a co-ed college, would she have become involved with Kevin? If she had dated men more worldly before he came along, would she have recognized the signs and identified Kevin as the deceiver he turned out to be and avoided the heartache?

Immaculata College was good; the total experience inspiring. Her father was ecstatic with her choice and with her achievements. She excelled academically, was president of the student body, sang in the college choir, played accordion in the college orchestra, played on both the volleyball and basketball teams and, for two years, edited the college yearbook.

Dating wasn't totally absent from her social life. She met a couple of young men with whom she had a good rapport, one an employee of her father; the other a friend of Michael's. Both were nice and she enjoyed their company. The problem was one worked for her father; the other was a friend of Michael's. She loved to dance, and both young men were good dancers.

Getting the vote of confidence from her father by bringing her into a business long seen as a "man's world" was a capstone of Traci's life. Everything she had worked for, sacrificed for, and prayed for, had come together. She was happy, enthusiastic, and held the world by its tail. What more could she want?

Then Kevin Sampson entered the picture.

CHAPTER TWELVE

THE Beetle Pension is located in the Vinohrady district of Prague, southeast of the National Museum and main train station. The name refers to the vineyards that grew here centuries ago; even as recently as 200 years ago there was little urbanization. Now the tree lined-streets are peppered with little cafés and bars. Vinohrady is one of the prettiest of Prague's inner suburbs. There isn't a lot to see, but walking along the Parisian-style streets is very pleasant.

Vinohrady's physical and commercial heart is Peace Square dominated by the brick neo-gothic St. Ludmilla Church, a popular meeting spot. Immediately behind the church is the neo-Renaissance National House with exhibitions and concert halls. On the northern side of the square is the 1909 Vinohrady Theater, a popular drama venue.

Bryce had assembled a three-day stay in Prague, reminiscent of the first visit he had made with Lauren. The first day would be spent walking through Old Town, the Jewish Quarter and across the Charles Bridge. On the second day they would go back across the bridge to the Prague Castle Area and Lesser Town. The third day would be set aside for museums, aimless meandering and shopping.

In choosing where to go and what to see, Bryce reread Lauren's journal account.

After checking into the Beetle Pension, we ate a meal put together from food we bought along the way from the Metro stop. We decided not to do a bus tour but rather a discovery walk. We went to Wenceslas Square and bought a dozen rolls of film. I could tell right away, this city will put a real dent in my film budget. We went by the Municipal Building and the Opera House to Town Market Square where we spent two hours or more looking, taking pictures, talking, and finding the centerpiece of the Square, the antique clock. Crowds! Beautiful buildings! Towers! We walked through Old Town

Square to the Charles Bridge to stroll and view the picturesque pan-
orama of the city and river. Artists and musicians were selling their
wares in both sides of the bridge's broad thoroughfare. I bought a
small watercolor print from an artist and a CD from a group play-
ing jazz. We took the Metro back to the Beetle. My camera never
stopped clicking.

"Even more than most cities in Europe, there is far more to see
in Prague than there's time for," Bryce explained to Traci. "So I've
picked the spots to visit that will give the best overview of the history and culture. Wherever we go, the architecture is eye-popping.
I think you'll love this place."

When entering into the Old Town Square the visitor steps back
in time 700 years. The air is permeated with history. This square
is one of two main squares in the center of the city, the other being
Wenceslas Square, located nearby. Dating back to the late 12th
century, Old Town started life as the marketplace for Prague. Over
the next few centuries, many buildings of Romanesque, Baroque
and Gothic styles were erected around the market, each bringing
with them stories of wealthy merchants and intrigue.

The square's most notable sights are the Church of Our Lady,
the Old Town Hall Tower and Astronomical Clock, and the magnificent St. Nicholas Church. In the center of the square is a stat-
ute of Jan Hus, erected in 1915 to mark the 500th anniversary of
the reformer's death. The groundswell of support for his beliefs
during the 14th and 15th centuries eventually led to the Hussite
Wars.

Stopping for lunch at a sidewalk café on the south side of the
square, Bryce's demeanor turned pensive.

"What are you thinking?" Traci asked. "Anything you can
share?"

"Just over there, across the street," Bryce explained, "Lauren
had her camera stolen from her shoulder bag. The thief was so
professional she didn't realize it was missing until she reached for
her camera to take a picture of the town hall. The joke was on the
thief though; the camera was ailing and it was going to be replaced
anyway."

"That's a good reminder for me to be more careful," Traci said.
"I'm sometimes cavalier about my bag and purse."

"When Lauren and I got back to the room – after buying a new
Olympus camera from a shop in Wenceslas Square – we found a

brochure with a warning saying something to the effect 'enjoy your visit, but beware of pickpockets. Some are so good they can steal the shoes off your feet.' We had a good laugh at how true that was."

Following a leisurely lunch Bryce suggested they stroll to the nearby Jewish Quarter, with a history going back to the 12th century. In the Quarter there is the oldest still-existing synagogue in Europe – the Old New Synagogue – and the Old Jewish Cemetery from the 15th century.

The first Jewish settlements in Prague were in existence in the 10th century, but the present area, known as Josefov, was settled during the last half of the 12th century. The Quarter was enclosed by a wall with six gates, which was a defense fortification intended to protect the Jews from attacks. There were anti-Jewish storms already in the 13th century, caused by edicts imposed by the Fourth Council of the Lateran (the biggest Catholic council of the Middle Ages) in 1215. However, the Jews in Prague were protected by the king, because they paid their taxes.

The year 1389 is one of the saddest dates in the history of Jews in Prague when the biggest anti-Jewish pogrom in the Middle Ages occurred. More than 3,000 citizens of the Quarter were massacred, their homes plundered and burned.

The status of Jews in Prague improved during the reign of Emperor Joseph II, but they had to stay in the Jewish ghetto and couldn't move anywhere else. In 1848 the Quarter was annexed as Prague's fifth town and was named Josefov in honor of Joseph II. After a time more affluent Jews moved from the city to other parts of Europe, Josefov became a place for poor people. Because of declining hygienic conditions the decision was made to demolish the Quarter, and that was done in 1897. Only a few valuable historic buildings were spared.

Today, there are six synagogues, the Jewish City Hall and the Old Jewish Cemetery. The Jewish Museum was founded in 1906 to preserve valuable historical and art objects rescued from the demolished houses and synagogues.

As they walked toward the Charles Bridge, Bryce asked a question that caught Traci off guard.

"Have you given much thought to the rest of your life?"

"My, you really are unpredictable," Traci replied. "What brought on that question?"

"I'm not sure. Maybe it has something to do with my hoping

you'll be staying around the Bay Area after the legal stuff's done. I can understand if you want to get out of Dodge. You don't have anything to keep you from going anywhere and doing anything your heart desires. Do you plan to keep teaching?"

"Bryce, could we talk about these things another time? Right now, I just want to enjoy today, and all the other todays until I leave for home. I'm curious about some things, too; but those can wait."

"Oh, great," Bryce said. "Now I'm curious about what you might be curious about."

"I'll share one thing I'm curious about," Traci said with a smile. "Would you take me dancing sometime?"

The Charles Bridge is on the top of every Prague visitor's list. It's alive with Czech artists, musicians, souvenir vendors whose stands line both sides of the bridge year-round. Bryce had selected the bridge for their last stop because the best time of day to come to the bridge is at sunset when there is a breathtaking view of the fully lit Prague Castle against the evening sky.

The Bridge is a stone Gothic structure which connects the Old Town and Mala Strana, also known as the Lesser Quarter. Its construction was ordered by Czech King Charles IV and began in 1357. In charge of construction was Peter Parier whose other works include the Cathedral at the Prague Castle. It's said that egg yolks were mixed into the mortar to strengthen the construction. Since the Bridge has survived many floods, most recently in August, 2002 when the country experienced the worst flood in 500 years, the egg yolks must not have been such a bad idea.

A total of 30 Baroque statues began to be placed on either side of the Bridge in the 17th century. The most popular statue is the one of St. John of Nepomuk, a Czech martyr saint who was executed during the reign of Wenceslas IV by being thrown into the Vitava River from the bridge. The plaque on the statue has been polished to a shine from people having touched it to bring good luck and ensure their return to Prague.

Bryce and Traci rubbed the plaque vigorously.

Getting off the tram as they returned from the Charles Bridge, mass was being held at St. Ludmilla Church, a beautiful building in their neighborhood and, to Traci's surprise, Bryce suggested they go inside. The service was in progress with the organ playing a stirring selection from Handel's Messiah. They slipped quietly into a rear pew.

The homily was delivered in a forceful, although singsong, manner. Unlike the mass in Metz, there was no printed English translation. At the close of the mass, Traci went forward to receive communion; Bryce sat and waited.

During the short walk from the church to the Beetle, neither spoke, seemingly lost in their separate thoughts. Within a block of their destination, Bryce took Traci's hand in his; she rested her head on his shoulder and their pace slowed.

At breakfast, Bryce reviewed the day's itinerary and offered a suggestion for the next day, their last in Prague. Today would start with the usual stroll to the tram station and then they would visit the Prague Castle area and Lesser Town. Tomorrow morning, Bryce would locate a laundromat and become "Mr. Super Suds" for washing their clothes as he was down to his cleanest dirty shirt and had been washing his socks in the bathroom sink. Traci could have a lazy morning. Then they would have lunch and go shopping.

"If you're not busy in the evening," Bryce said, trying to appear and sound sophomoric, "I'd like to take you out on a date."

"That sounds interesting," Traci answered, picking up on Bryce's role playing. "Oh no, I forgot. Tomorrow night is when I do my nails."

Prague Castle is the largest medieval castle complex in Europe and was the ancient seat of Czech kings through the ages. The Castle complex consists of St. Vitus Cathedral – the most recognizable landmark in the city – viewing towers, museums and art galleries, a monastery, several palaces – including Lubkowicz Palace – and St. George's Basilica, a popular venue for early evening classical concerts.

The first known building on the site of the Castle was erected in the 9th century. During the 12th century this building was replaced by a Romanesque palace. In the 14th century that palace was rebuilt in the Gothic style under Charles IV. Another reconstruction took place during the reign of King Vladislav Jagiello at the end of the 15th century.

Resulting from a fire in 1541, the Castle underwent further renovation. The Spanish Hall was added during the reign of Rudolf II and final alterations were made by Empress Maria Theresa. Today, the Castle is the seat of the president of the Czech Republic and serves as the historical and political of both the city and the state.

Bryce's schedule was set to assure Traci and he would be at the front gates before noon to watch the Changing of the Guard. While this ceremony takes place every hour, at noon there is more fanfare.

"Before we begin touring the Castle and cathedral," Bryce said, "we need to buy a photo permit so we can take pictures."

"I've never heard of that requirement anywhere," Traci replied. "What's the purpose?"

"They use the revenue for upkeep on the buildings, I imagine. We'll be given a stick-on badge to wear showing the security force we have a license to take pictures."

Following their two-hour exploration, they wandered down to Mala Strana, more commonly known as Lesser Town, which clusters at the foot of the Castle. This part of the city got its start in the 8th century as a market settlement and was nearly destroyed twice – during the Hussite Wars in 1419 and in the Great Fire of 1541.

The most intriguing street in the Town is Neruda Way, a part of the bustling Royal Way, and is an architectural delight. Many of its Renaissance facades have been 'baroquefied'; many still have their original shutter-like doors, while others are adorned with emblems. Number 47 is the House of Two Suns where the Czech poet Jan Neruda lived from 1845 to 1891.

At the intersection with Jansky Street is Bretfeld Palace, which Josef Bretfeld made a center for social gatherings in 1765. Among his guests were Mozart and Casanova.

Of all the baroque churches throughout Europe, there is none more spectacular than the Church of St. Nicholas, Mala Strana's primary landmark. The ceiling fresco by Johann Kracker in 1770 is the largest in Europe. Up a flight of stairs is a gallery housing Skreta's gloomy 17th century Passion Cycle paintings.

Nearby is the Old Town Hall where in 1575 the non-Catholic nobles wrote the 'Czech Confession', a pioneering demand for religious tolerance eventually passed into law by Rudolf II in 1609. In practice the demands were not fully met, and the nobles eventually got angry enough to fling two Hapsburg councilors out of a castle window.

———

Bryce had bundled the clothes to be laundered and packed them into his rolling suitcase for his trek to a laundromat, a half-dozen blocks from the Beetle. He enjoyed the challenge of figuring out how to make the variety of European machines work since – at least it seemed to him – no two facilities have similar operating instructions. He also enjoyed being helpful to other tourists who enter the establishments and stand mystified, looking confused trying to understand how the process works.

The washing and drying chore took almost two hours. When he got back to the Beetle, Bryce found Traci sitting in front of the computer composing an email to Michael.

"I'm on the third draft," she confessed. "There's so much I want to share with him, but I read what I've written and realize it's probably much more than I should be telling. I'd like to assure him Bishop Grogan won't cause any trouble, and then I think that's premature until we hear from Zach Tillson. Could you help me out?"

"I'll be glad to give it a try. Take the clothes up and get ready to go out for lunch and our shopping spree and I'll have something for you to review when you get back."

When Traci returned, she looked radiant. For the past couple of days, her smile had changed in frequency from occasionally to almost always.

"How about something like this for Michael?" Bryce handed her a printout of a draft email.

My dearest Michael,

This is a note to let you know I'm alive and well. I appreciated the email regarding your concern over my current dispute with Bishop Grogan. The Bishop and I have communicated and I'm confident we can come to an amicable understanding which, hopefully, will lead to quieting the waters.

I'm still in Europe for an indefinite time and not sure when I'll be returning to SF. I'll keep you posted. In the meantime I'll have you in my prayers and thoughts; please keep me in yours.

I do love you, big brother. – Cait

"How do you do that?" Tracy asked. "How can you get inside my head and have me say the words I need to say with such directness and sensitivity?"

"We're simpatico," Bryce answered. "Now, let's send this and go have lunch."

It was an easygoing afternoon. Bryce bought a few small souvenirs for his office staff and mailed an obligatory picture postcard to Sharon, his assistant. Traci was faced with the realization she had no one to buy anything for, or to even send a card. This didn't deter her, however, from buying a few gifts for herself as she was dazzled by Czech crystal and amber jewelry. The more time they spent with each other, the easier it was to laugh, to joke, to trade puns.

They returned to the Beetle to begin the process of getting ready to leave the next morning, and sprucing for the evening out. Bryce said he would be at her door promptly at seven, "If you have your nails done by then" and he knew the perfect dancing spot.

True to his word, at the stroke of seven o'clock he knocked on Traci's door and she immediately opened it. As they stood looking at each other, it was a magical moment. Traci was resplendent in the khaki pants and white Marrakesh tunic she bought at Harrods; her long red hair hung soft and naturally over her shoulders. Bryce complimented her outfit with his blue Tarragon sport coat and off-white Dockers pants. His button-down white shirt collar was open at the top, revealing a gold chain around his neck.

"Our chariot awaits," Bryce announced, offering Traci his arm and escorting her to a reserved taxi parked at the curb in front of the Beetle.

"The Karlovy Lazne," he instructed the driver.

The Karlovy Lazne is one of the coolest places in Prague if you're into serious clubbing. One entrance fee gets you a ticket to five clubs on five levels. Each floor has its own style, from chill out to hard-core trance. The five levels consists of the entrance level Music Café, Discotheque for lovers of disco, Kaleidoscope covering hits from the '60s to the '80s, the Paradogs Club for the best of house, trance and techno, and finally a chill out zone in the top floor café, playing a mellow selection of music and featuring cushions, rugs and soft lighting.

Traci wanted to spend time on each level, and Bryce agreed, with the condition they had more time for the Kaleidoscope level than any of the others. The evening proved to be one of the best either could remember. Both were excellent dancers and Bryce enjoyed singing along as they moved gracefully to many of the classics, including Bridge Over Troubled Waters, Killing Me Softly With His Song, and Sunshine On My Shoulder.

The evening was over far too soon. Their last dance before leaving was to Bill Withers signature song, Lean On Me. During the ride back to the Beetle, they sat close together in the taxi. Bryce walked Traci to her door; she unlocked it and looked deeply into his eyes. He took her face gently in the palms of his hands and softly kissed her warm lips.

"Good night, lovely lady."

"Good night, kind sir."

"Have a restful night. Tomorrow we go to Budapest."

CHAPTER THIRTEEN

TRAVEL time from Prague to Budapest is eight hours, including a half-hour stop in Bratislava, the capital of Slovakia. With the departure time set for eleven thirty, Bryce expected Traci to sleep in. But to his surprise she knocked on his door at seven forty five.

"Are you decent?" she asked before Bryce opened the door.

"I will be in a second," Bryce responded, quickly pulling on his pants. He opened the door to find Traci, luggage in tow, standing in the hallway. He moved to kiss her good morning, but before he could, she gave him a quick peck on the cheek as she entered the room.

"We didn't set a time for leaving this morning," she said. "So I thought I'd better get with the program. Rather than having breakfast here in the Beetle, how about I treat at that quaint little bistro across from the station?"

"That work's for me," Bryce said. "We won't miss the train if we're already there."

As they were checking out, Bryce requested the desk clerk call for a taxi to take them to the station.

"My gracious," Traci said. "Taxis two days in a row. What have I done to deserve this?"

"Nothing . . . and everything," Bryce responded without explanation.

The morning sky was a bit grey and overcast so they decided to go inside the bistro rather than sit at a sidewalk table. The usual Czech breakfast includes white bread or rolls, cold cuts, cheese and hard-boiled eggs, washed down with tea, coffee or hot chocolate. Meals are never rushed, either in the serving or the eating.

Conversation quickly turned to the night before, with Traci taking the lead.

"Thanks again for the wonderful time. You're a great dancer – and singer. I noticed a few times, couples close to us would stop dancing and listen to you sing. You must know the words to every

Top 40 hit from the '70s."

"I do know quite a few. They don't write songs like that anymore, and it's too bad."

"Was dancing a big part of your social life when you were in college?"

"Not so much. Once a month or so our fraternity would sponsor a dance and I'd usually show up for those. They were all stag so I didn't have to worry about getting a date. Most of my dancing came after I met Lauren. She loved to dance and thought I needed to have more fun. We even belonged to a dance club for awhile when we were first married."

"Did you date anyone seriously before Lauren came into your life?"

"There were a couple of great girls I thought I could get serious with, and there was one who got very serious about me. Her name was Sandra Warren. People thought we were the perfect couple. We graduated from high school together and we both went to the University of Washington. Her parents and my parents were good friends so we did a lot of things together like, you know, barbecues or sailing on her father's boat. A lot of planning was being done that made me uncomfortable. People were making plans for me rather than with me."

"Knowing you as I'm learning to know you tells me someone was trying to fly the proverbial lead balloon," Traci offered.

"Yeah," Bryce chuckled, "that someone was Sandra's mom. After a while things got sorted out and Sandra even admitted she was hoping for too much too fast. Less than a year after we stopped dating, Sandra was married to a great guy and both Sandra and her mother were happy."

"Something struck me yesterday when we were shopping," Traci said in a serious tone. "After I decided to commit my life to other people, I really haven't had much of a life. It was suddenly startling when I couldn't think of anyone to whom I might send a postcard, let alone buy a present. Strange, but aside from the other members of my order, I have no friends. And I wouldn't count any of those women as a close friend."

"You have Michael," Bryce reminded her.

"Yes, and I thank God for him every day. That's why it's so important for me to keep him close. So tell me, who's your best friend?"

"Sadly, since Lauren died I don't have one. There are a number of acquaintances and business colleagues who I know will be there to lend a hand if I need help. But there's no one who would give me the shirt off his back."

"I fell asleep last night trying to remember the words to Bill Withers Lean on Me. You sang it so beautifully. I won't ask you to sing here, but could you speak the words?"

"Gladly, lovely lady. May I hold your hand?"

"You may hold both of them," Traci smiled.

> Sometimes in our lives we all have pain
> We all have sorrow
> But if we are wise
> We know that there's always tomorrow
> Lean on me when you're not strong
> And I'll be your friend
> I'll help you carry on
> For it won't be long
> 'Til I'm gonna need
> Somebody to lean on
> Please swallow your pride
> If I have things you need to borrow
> For no one can fill those of your needs
> That you won't let show
> If there is a load you need to bear
> That you can't carry
> I'm right up the road
> I'll share your load
> If you just call on me
> So just call on me brother, when you need a hand
> We all need somebody to lean on
> I just might have a problem that you'd understand
> We all need somebody to lean on

When Bryce finished reciting the lyrics, mascara tears ran down Traci's face. She leaned across the table, kissed the lips of her friend, and smiled.

———————

Rumbling through the eastern region of the Czech Republic,

watching the changing landscape, it becomes visually apparent when the train crosses the border into Slovakia. The countryside remains the same, but the state of the economy between the two countries is in stark contrast.

Lauren noted in her journal:

While there are a lot of similarities in types of housing and styles between the CR and Slovakia, we get a very strong impression that Czech's are considerably tidier than are Slovs. Even the fields here show signs of less attention than in CR. Lots of trash dumped in various places in the woods and along the tracks. Not all along, certainly, but far more than other European countries.

Every now and again we see pretty (though plain and drab) villages nestled by the woods. Farm equipment looks old and rusty. There are very few cars, almost all at least twenty years old.

Bratislava, the capital, is somewhat better maintained than the rural areas. But of course we only know what we could see from our vantage point on the train and in the station. It's a very large city and spread out. Our conductor pointed to an impressive palace on the hill and suggested we should to take pictures, which I did as we left Bratislava. The closer we got to the Hungarian border, the garden plots and greenhouses seemed to improve considerably.

Budapest came into being in 1873 with the merging of three separate towns. Buda was a hilly residential community; Pest was a flat industrial area; the historic Obuda was situated to the north of Buda. The beautiful Danube River separated Pest from Buda and Obuda in its meandering 1,780 mile sojourn from the confluence of the Brigach and Breg Rivers in Germany to its discharge into the Black Sea.

At the time of the Mongol invasion in 1241 the town of Pest, because it was built on a plain was completely defenseless and was burned down and its population massacred. The citizens who were spared considered it safer to build a new town, protected by ramparts, on a steep limestone plateau. They named the new town Buda. The Royal Castle was built at the southern end of the plateau and the civilian town to the north.

Until the early 1700's the former town of Pest lay fallow. Slowly it began to rebuild and grow; however, on the site of the original town of Pest there remain only some sections of the 15th century town walls along with the churches and a few public buildings.

Today the area is recognized as the Inner City of Budapest and, in contrast to the Castle District of Buda which is bypassed by the city's main traffic, the Inner City with its shops and offices is the pulse of the city's everyday life.

Bryce was confident they would be able to find lodging in a once-grand, but now somewhat dilapidated hotel across a broad boulevard adjacent to the train station where he and Lauren had stayed on their last trip to Budapest. Falling back into an old pattern, he left Traci in the station café to guard the luggage while he set about to rediscover the hotel and check for vacancies. Within 20 minutes he was back at the station with a look on his face resembling a Cheshire cat that had just eaten a canary.

"What are you looking so pleased about?" Traci asked. "Did you find the hotel?"

"I found the hotel, but it wasn't the hotel," Bryce said, smiling even more broadly. "The hotel I was remembering had a well-worn look with clean, but shabby, drapes and furniture. There was no food service and the bathrooms were down the hall. The hotel I found in its place is one resulting from a three-year total reconstruction and refurbishment. Only the exterior façade is the same as I remember. Its new name is the Golden Park Hotel. Here's a brochure."

Traci read out loud. "The Golden Park offers 172 elegant rooms equipped with air-conditioning, sound proof windows, bathrooms, color TV with satellite channels, telephone, safe, fridge, electronic key-card system, smoke detector, automatic wake-up system."

"There's more stuff on the back," Bryce said.

"That's enough for me," Traci admitted, then read the reverse side. "Other services include laundry and ironing facility, lobby bar, Mediterranean and Italian restaurants, souvenir shop, sauna and massage."

"What do you think?" Bryce asked.

"I think it sounds perfectly wonderful. It's been years since I had a real massage."

"I think it's great, too," Bryce agreed. "Makes me sorry they don't have any vacancies."

The disappointed look on Traci's face caused Bryce to quickly admit he was joking and produced their room key cards. A feeling inside that he was beginning to regain his sense of humor was rewarding.

It was late when they settled into their rooms and both ready to relax. After a light dinner of salads in the Mediterranean restaurant, Bryce saw Traci to her room and said good night without going inside. He would work on the Budapest itinerary and have it ready to discuss at breakfast. Traci had a couple of books from London and looked forward to an evening of reading.

To his surprise, and mild consternation, Bryce began feeling a growing anxiety about this trip which was to be serious and somber, designed to be introspective and focus on his sorrow over the death of Lauren until all the pain was rinsed from his spirit. He wasn't supposed to be having fun.

In a city as large and beautifully diverse as Budapest, it's difficult to select which places to visit and which to merely see while walking past or looking down on from a hillside vantage point. This was Bryce's fourth time in the city; it would be Traci's first and – perhaps – only chance to see it all. With this in mind, Bryce chose to devote most of their time in and around the Castle district in Buda; the Chain Bridge; walks through the Inner City, including Little Boulevard; Margaret Island and the City Park. And on the Pest side, the Parliament and the Plaza with its upscale shops.

If it proved to be impossible to see all this in the three days allotted, at least they'd give it the old college try. Bryce was wishing he could let Traci know he would be very willing to change any part of their remaining schedule to make sure she saw what she wanted to see, not just what was on the fixed itinerary. Remembering that discretion is the better part of valor, he decided not to revisit the subject.

After an early breakfast, during which Bryce outlined the day's activities, they made their way to the Metro, located in the train station complex and headed for Buda.

The Castle District in Buda is the ancient kernel of the capital's right-bank settlement. Everything that surrounds it was once only suburbs. From whatever direction, to reach the Castle District, the ramparts which completely encircle Castle Hill must be crossed. The entire area within the ramparts is protected as a monument; the lines of the streets and the foundations and architectural remains of the buildings retain the atmosphere and memories of the medieval and 18th and 19th century capital.

The Fishermen's Bastion is one of the most popular spots for visitors to the Castle District. It offers a grand panorama of almost the entire city. The Bastion's architecture with its flights of stairs, its projections, its turrets and its galleries make it a mixture of neo-Gothic and neo-Romanesque styles. Besides the unique, captivating beauty of this place, from the Bastion is a breathtaking view of the Danube, Pest and the parliament buildings.

The Fishermen's Bastion got its name from the medieval ramparts system which rose above the suburb called Fishermen's Town. Beneath the Bastion lies the old suburb of Water Town, now full of modern buildings with only its Baroque church towers recalling the past.

The building dominating the panorama of the Pest bank is the Parliament with its many domes and spires. At the head of the Chain Bridge in Pest the impressive building housing the Hungarian Academy of sciences can be seen, with the dome of the Basilica in the background. The church towers between the Chain Bridge, built in 1849, and the 1964 Elizabeth Bridge are reminders of the past Inner City of Pest. The panorama ends at the dolomite rocks of Gellert Hill.

In the upper court of the Fishermen's Bastion stands an equestrian statue of Steven I, the first king of Hungary and founder of the State. Just below the Bastion, in a bend of the road stands the impressive statue of Janos Hunyadi, father of the future King Matthias. Hunyadi was a famous military commander who, in 1465, repulsed the Turkish attack on what is today Belgrade. Not far away there is a replica of the famous statue of St. George by the Kolozsvari brothers. The 1373 original can be seen in Prague.

It was early afternoon before Bryce's growling stomach let him know it was past time for lunch. Traci was ready for a stop as well and as soon as they were seated inside the classy Ruszwurm Café she slipped her shoes off and let out a sigh of relief.

"I hope I'll be able to get these back on," she said. "My feet feel two times larger than my shoes. I guess it's a fair trade off. All this walking may be hard on my feet, but the calories I burn will help take the fat off."

Bryce had learned at an early age if a woman uses the word 'fat' in a sentence about herself, it's not something a man should respond to. So he kept to himself the questioning thought as to which part of her well-proportioned body she considered 'fat'.

The first visit after lunch was to be The Church of Our Lady and then a walk across the Chain Bridge to the Pest side of the river.

"When we're up and moving again, maybe we should find an Internet Café and check for emails," Bryce suggested.

"You can check with your office, but I'm not going to check for emails," Traci responded. "I don't want to be reminded of that part of the world, not while we're having such a good time. If there is a bad-news message, I can't do anything about it right away; if it's a good-news message, there would be no need to answer. I'm going to wait until Salzburg before checking."

"Of course. I'm really glad your anxiety level is getting lower. For the past few days you've seemed more relaxed and even smile a lot. By the way, you have a beautiful smile."

The Church of Our Lady is more commonly called the Matthias Church because its southern tower bears the coat of arms with the raven of Matthias Hunyadi, born in 1458 and died in 1490. In the 13th century Buda's first parish church stood on the site. In the 14th century it was rebuilt as a Gothic hall church, but its construction – just as that of so many Gothic churches in Europe – was never finished, and the northern tower was not built.

In Turkish times it became the main mosque and its interior furnishings were destroyed. During the 1686 siege its tower and roof collapsed. The church was rebuilt as Baroque and in the last years of the 19th century it was reconstructed, using as its footprint the excavated medieval remains and the original Gothic church. The last two kings of Hungary were Francis Joseph I in 1876 and Charles IV in 1916.

From outside, the most beautiful part of the church is the 260 foot high stone-laced Gothic tower. The southern portal is decorated by a 14th century relief depicting the Virgin Mary's death. Inside, the plastered walls are painted with colored ornamental designs. Near the chancel, in a former crypt, there is a stonework museum, including medieval carvings. In the gallery a collection of ecclesiastical art is exhibited, containing old chalices and vestments as well as a replica of the crown of the Hungarian kings.

During World War II the damage suffered by the church was so heavy it took two decades to repair.

Opposite the Church of Our Lady is the former Town Hall of Buda which now houses a research institute. On the corner of the building stands the statue of Pallas Athene, the patron of the town, holding the coat of arms of Buda. The Baroque Trinity Statue in the center of the square was erected by the citizens in the 18th century in thanksgiving for their escape from the plague.

From the center of Castle Hill four parallel streets run due north and two run due south. The streets of the district are sometimes broken by bends or slopes allowing only parts to be seen at a time. Owing to the influence of Italian architecture, the tops of the houses run parallel to the axis of the streets, which results in a restful and harmonious picture.

Even on newer facades it's common to find medieval door and window frames, frescoes or upper floors projecting on arches, and niches with seats in the doorways. While no explanation can be given for this last feature of the architecture of medieval Buda, it's assumed that the servants of guests visiting the noblemen and wealthy citizens would wait in these niches for their masters.

Starting their return to the hotel from Castle Hill, taking the tram down the steep hillside, Bryce and Traci walked hand-in-hand across the Chain Bridge to Pest. The construction of the bridge took ten years, from 1839 to 1849, and was inspired by Count Istvan Szechenyi, one of the greatest figures of the Reform Period. Szechenyi, whom Lajos Kossuth called 'the greatest Hungarian', encouraged the nation, groaning under foreign oppression to build factories, mills, roads and bridges.

The Chain Bridge, 420 yards long and 17 yards wide, is supported by pillars shaped like antique triumphal arches. It was the first bridge built across the Danube and not only linked Buda with Pest but also the western with the eastern parts of the country. In January 1945 Hitler's troops blew up the bridge, but in 1948 it was rebuilt in its original form.

———————————

Back at the hotel, smooth jazz was being played in the lobby bar. They ordered a bottle of Hungarian Tokay wine and a variety of canapés including Piquant Hungarian salami, crab with dill sauce, sun dried tomatoes with Emmental cheese and smoked veal with pickles.

"What a wonderful day," Traci said enthusiastically. "My muscles ache, my feet are sore, I don't even want to look in a mirror for fear I'll scream; but it was a truly remarkable day."

"Traci, I know I have a bad habit of repeating myself. I want to

tell you again how fortunate I am to have met you and how grateful I am that you decided to come along. It's a blessing."

"And for me, too," Traci responded softly, squeezing Bryce's
arm. "I shudder to think how I would have handled my situation
left to my own devices. I've thought many times about the circumstances of our meeting and truly believe it was God's doing. He
put us on the same plane, arranged our seating assignments and
even, I believe, helped us be comfortable talking to each other."

"That's a nice thought," Bryce concurred. "I'm not so sure God
took time from His busy schedule to look after us personally. Maybe our guardian angels met at the airport, compared notes, and
decided their jobs would be easier if they joined forces. But whatever made it happen – accidentally or by design – I'm very glad."

Traci stopped by the reception desk and asked the procedure
for getting a massage. The accommodating clerk arranged an appointment for a masseuse to be available at the hotel spa in an
hour.

"That's perfect," she told Bryce. "I'll be able to shower and wash
this matted mop before going to the spa. Should I make an appointment for you when she's through with me?"

"No thanks. I'll be dead to the world in an hour. To be honest,
I've never had a professional massage. Lauren would rub my feet
sometimes, but that's as close to a massage I've been."

When they reached Traci's room, Bryce stepped inside for a moment, just long enough to share an embrace and a soft, lingering kiss.

———————

"How was the massage?" Bryce asked as soon as he opened his
door, responding to Traci's morning knock.

"Utterly divine," Traci cooed, "I feel like a spoiled and pampered
rag doll. The masseuse's name is Beata; she's from Poland and
speaks very little English. For a large woman, she has a gentle
touch and really knows her stuff. She found muscles I had no
idea were even a part of my body. You really should give it a try;
I know you'd like it."

During breakfast Bryce gave an overview of the remaining two
days in Budapest. They would do a walking tour of Obuda, spend
time on the Little Boulevard that encircles the Inner City, get tickets for a guided tour of the Parliament building and, finally, visit
City Park.

Obuda was the original Buda before the castle district was built and is the oldest section of the city. While Obuda doesn't have the picturesque ambiance of either Buda or Pest, it has a much longer history. There are well preserved Roman ruins – an amphitheater of the Roman Military Town and Roman baths in Florian Square – an early Christian graveyard, an ancient silk mill and textile museum, and the Zichy Castle.

Little Boulevard runs along the line of the former city walls and leads to Liberty Bridge. The most beautiful building on the Little Boulevard is the National Museum. In front of the façade, in the garden, stands the statue of Janos Arany, the great epic poet of the 19th century.

The 19th century Parliament Building is situated on Pest's riverbank and is a symbol of Hungary's independence. After the Austro-Hungarian Compromise in 1867, in which a dual monarchy was created, Hungary received additional independence and the country wrote its own constitution. It also initiated the creation of a Parliament Building. A competition for the project was officially started by the emperor Franz Joseph. The Parliament was built between 1885 and 1902, at the time the largest parliamentary building in the world. The main style of the building is neo-Gothic with renaissance influences, but the base ground plan is Baroque. A strong Byzantine affect is noticeable in the interior of the building, especially in the marvelously decorated staircase hall. The soaring dome and towers of the monumental Parliament gives a good counterweight to the Buda Castle on the opposite bank of the Danube.

The area of today's Budapest City Park was once a swamp where the Hungarian kings were elected between the 13th and 16th centuries. It was also a favorite hunting ground for the elite. The swamp had been drained and transformed into an English-style park in the 18th and 19th centuries when the emperor ordered the establishment of green space where people could relax and entertain. The park is now home to the Zoo, the Municipal Circus and the Amusement Park. An artificial lake is used for rowing in the summer and becomes a skating rink in the winter. Surrounding the lake there is a wooded area and a children's playground. On a small island in the lake stands an interesting group of buildings – the Vajdahunyad Castle. Budapest City Park was among the first public parks in the world open to people for relaxation purposes.

––––––––––––––––

"I hope we've spent enough time here for you to get the feel of

Budapest and the Hungarian people," Bryce said as he and Traci ordered their last dinner before preparing to leave the following morning for Salzburg. "I wanted to save the best meal for tonight. We can't leave Hungary without having goulash. In fact, I don't believe you're allowed out of the country without proof of having eaten it."

"Do you mean if we don't order goulash, we don't have to leave?" Traci asked. "If that's the case, I'll have roasted venison again."

"I could spend a whole two weeks here," Bryce said, sounding a little melancholy. "There's something about this city that speaks to me. I believe I mentioned it was a picture of Budapest I saw in a geography book as a school kid that planted the wanderlust seed in my brain. I'm sure this isn't my last trip here."

"What's on for tomorrow?" Traci asked with an air of enthusiasm.

"We'll be in Salzburg by bed time, assuming we can find beds when we get there," Bryce jokingly replied. "But I want to talk to you about how we get there. I'd like for us to take the hydrofoil up the Danube from here to Vienna and then the train from Vienna to Salzburg. This is something Lauren and I talked about on our last trip, but didn't do. I had the desk clerk call for reservations and we're set to board at nine in the morning if you're game."

Traci flashed her trademark smile. "What would you expect, silly man? Of course I'm game. What a treat. I'd love it!"

"Then let's have our goulash and go to our rooms. I have an appointment with Beata in less than an hour."

CHAPTER FOURTEEN

THE hydrofoil carries a maximum of 104 passengers with each airline-type seat equipped with consoles and earphones for listening to a recorded tour guide in a choice of languages. The boat also has a snack bar with a variety of cold food and drinks.

During the six hours on the Danube from Budapest to Vienna, Bryce and Traci discovered the beautiful cities and landscapes from a viewpoint available only to birds and sailors. Ports-of-call on the route included Vac, Esztergon, Komarom, and Bratislava before terminating in Vienna.

In the taxi rushing from the Vienna dock to the Vienna West train station, Bryce reminded Traci, "You can add another country to your collection; we're in Austria now."

As projected the train pulled into the Salzburg station a few minutes after six, in the late afternoon. Bryce agreed with Traci that the package of Pringle's potato chips and Snickers candy bars they had on the boat were inadequate for their day's nutritional needs. A hearty dinner would be their reward for hustling to get to Salzburg before dark. Putting into play their "Traci-guard/Bryce-find-rooms" routine, Bryce headed, literally running, to check the availability at the Pension Adlerhof, two blocks from the station. He returned with his patented tell-tale grin signifying he, once again, had beaten the odds.

An hour later they were seated in the comfort of a nearby restaurant noshing on a Bavarian version of a chef salad and downing a pitcher of Marzen beer. Traci was interested in the history of the city.

Salzburg can be regarded as the oldest and most important cultural and spiritual center in present-day Austria. Although it had already been elevated to the rank of archdiocese in 798 and from the late Middle Ages onward had formed a spiritual principality in the Holy Roman Empire, Salzburg is one of the youngest provinces. The development of the region and its ultimate separation from Bavaria, its mother country, was agreed to in the 14th century. But it wasn't until 1816, that Salzburg was incorporated into Austria. Of today's provinces, Salzburg is the only one to have been ruled by a prince-archbishop as an independent state and is the only one of the many spiritual principalities of the Holy Roman Empire still existing as an independent province.

The name Salzburg literally means "Salt Castle" and derives its name from the barges carrying salt on the Salzach River.

"Of course, Salzburg's best known native son was Mozart," Bryce said. "Tomorrow we'll visit his birthplace and his residence. One of the advantages of being a tourist here is the compactness of the city. It's relatively small compared to other places we've been, so it's pretty easy to see and do a lot of things in a short period of time."

"How many days will we be here?" Traci asked.

"I'm thinking two full days at least. I want you to see much of what Old Town has to offer and also walk through some pretty spectacular places outside Old Town like the grounds and Palace of Mirabell."

"Sounds like a plan," Traci said.

"And we really should check for emails in the morning. Our hotel doesn't have a computer for public use, but there's an Internet Cafe near the train station. We can't go now; it closes early evening."

"That works for me. I'm pretty bushed."

It was almost nine thirty before Traci knocked on Bryce's door letting him know she was up and about. They were too late for breakfast in the hostel but found coffee and pastries on the way to the Internet Café. Once there, Bryce signed in for a computer. He quickly checked his email and found one had been sent by Zach Tillson, Bishop Grogan's lawyer. He opened the message.

Dear Bryce,

What a delightful surprise it was for me to get your email and find you represent Sister Teresa! It's always easier for me to work with someone I already know and respect. I was so sorry to learn of your wife's untimely death. I apologize for not getting in touch with you to offer my condolences. Please accept them now.

As to the matter at hand, I've had numerous lengthy discussions

with my client and I'm sorry to report he still is in no mood to con-
cede that he is culpable in any matter regarding Sister Teresa. It's
unfortunate that neither she nor you are available to engage per-
sonally in meaningful dialog. I truly hope this can happen sooner
rather than later.

My client has asked me to convey a message to you and Sister
Teresa. This is a verbatim quote, "Let's just get this nonsense over
with."

On the other issue, however, concerning Father Michael Dunn,
my client has assured me he will not play the role of obstructionist
in any way relating to Father Dunn's pending appointment in New
Jersey. I also advised him against sending any further messages
directly to Sister Teresa. He agrees he shouldn't be feeding the dog
that might someday bite him in the rear. It goes without saying,
now that she has attorney representation, I will desist in contacting
her as well.

I'm eager to know your plans. While, fortunately, time is not of
the essence in this matter, I too would like to get this all behind us
in an expeditious manner.

My very best regards,
Zach Tillson

Bryce chuckled as he printed the message and handed it to
Traci. "Seems like we're having a lot more fun than Bishop Grogan. In his lawyerlike manner, Zach is telling me the good Bishop
is really bugging him and ol' Zach is pleading to us for mercy."

"Are you going to answer now?" Traci asked.

"No. I'll work on a response while we're on the train to Florence."

Bryce turned the keyboard over to Traci. Her inbox showed she
had a message from Michael, sent two days after her last contact.
She stared at the screen for a moment.

"I'm not sure I want to read this, but here goes."

My darling Cait,

I'm asking your forgiveness for the way I railed on you concern-
ing what is happening between you and Bishop Grogan. I was to-
tally out of line. Instead of waiting to hear your version of the story
as I should have, I chose to side with a man I don't even know –
simply because of his office. It was selfish on my part to make this
situation all about me. If it's in God's plan for me to get the Trenton
appointment then I will, despite what anyone thinks can be done to
prevent it.

I love you, little sister, wherever you may be. I pray every day for God's hand to guide you in both body and soul. – Michael

Bryce noticed a decidedly improved energy level in Traci after she received Michael's note of apology. Not that she had been dragging around, but with the weight of being concerned about Michael's appointment lifted, there was a spring in her step and a lilt in her voice that hadn't been there before. He began to wonder how truly vibrant she must be when she has no pressing worries. That question couldn't be answered until they returned home and settled the score with Clifton Norton.

Like it had been in all the places on their itinerary they had visited, one of the most difficult decisions was determining the best things to see or do to the exclusion of everything else. To do justice, each should be a stand-alone destination site. Given the time and circumstances of this trip, however, made the 'Whitman's Sampler' scenario the only feasible one. Now, to further acerbate the schedule, Bryce was starting to wrestle with how to shorten it without being struck by a Tracibolt.

It's an easy, casual walk from Pension Adlerhof across the river to Mozartplatz in the center of Old Town. Towering above the city from almost anywhere, the most formidable sight is the Hohensalzburg Fortress. As well as being the icon of Salzburg, it is the largest fortress of its kind in Europe to have survived intact in its entirety. But for Traci, it was the beauty of a dozen or more churches in Old Town and along the river that captured her attention and nonstop picture taking.

The fortress was built by Archbishop Gebhard in 1077 and expanded extensively by Archbishop Leonhard von Keutschach over a 22 year period from 1495 to 1519. Today, its greatest attractions are the medieval Princes' Chambers and the Fortress Museum. A short funicular railway provides a convenient way up the steep ascent.

Ornamental paintings and crafted Gothic carvings can be seen and admired in the Golden Hall and the Golden Room. Fifty-eight inscriptions and the famous coat of arms are additional reminders of the years Bishop von Keutschach ruled. The last significant modification to the fortress was the construction of the impressive Khuenburg bastion in 1681.

On the north side of Old Town stands the beautiful Mirabell

Palace, with a fascinating history. In 1606, Prince Archbishop Wolf Dietrich von Raitenau commissioned a palace built outside the city walls for his lover, Salome Alt. He called the palace 'Altenau' and was intended to be a fitting residence for Salome and their children. Since von Raitenau was a cleric, he was forbidden to marry; nonetheless, Salome bore him 15 children, ten of whom survived.

The palace was given its current name by Wolf Dietrich's successor, Markus Sittikus. After the death of Wolf Dietrich, who was forced to abdicate in 1612 and held prisoner in Hohensalzburg Fortress where he died, Sittikus renamed the palace 'Mirabell'.

Within the palace, a large room named the Marble Hall once served as the ceremonial venue for the Prince Archbishops, is now one of the most beautiful wedding halls in the world. Leopold Mozart and his children, Wolfgang and Nanneri, performed here numerous times for aristocrats attending festive dinners. The Marble Hall is also an imposing location for conferences, ceremonies and atmospheric concerts.

Also today, the palace houses the offices of Salzburg's mayor and town council.

In a house located at No. 9 Getreidegasse is where Wolfgang Amadeus Mozart was born on January 27, 1756. The rooms on the third floor which were occupied by the Mozart family are now a museum. Mementoes, including the young Mozart's violin, portraits, a 1760 clavichord, a 1780 pianoforte and volumes of musical scores can be seen.

On the second floor is an interesting exhibition, "Mozart in the Theater," with illuminated miniature stages. Mozart's father Leopold, who occupied the house from 1747 to 1753, was an excellent violinist and music teacher who for many years beginning in 1762 took Wolfgang and his sister, who was five years older, on concert tours throughout Europe during which time the youthful Mozart gained great acclaim for his virtuoso piano playing.

Wolfgang Amadeus Mozart died under mysterious circumstances in Vienna on December 5, 1791, just a few weeks shy of his 35th birthday. No one knows for certain where he was buried. A tragic ending for such an industrious life.

————————

It had been a quick two days of soaking up and drinking in as much of Salzburg's history and culture as that amount of time would allow. Bryce had given Traci the opportunity to decide if she wanted them to take the "Sound of Music" tour and, much to his relief, it wasn't high on her list.

They chose instead, as their Salzburg finale, to return to the gardens of Mirabell Palace and stroll among the flowers and manicured shrubs. To their delight, a wedding ceremony was just concluding in the Marble Hall and as the pipe organ played a rousing recessional, the newlyweds emerged and walked to a gleaming white carriage with two perfectly-matched white horses listening for their driver's command to go. A liveried footman helped the happy middle-aged couple into the carriage, took his place alongside the driver and they were off, to the cheers of their friends.

"How beautiful was that?" asked Traci.

"Almost as beautiful as you," Bryce answered. "But not quite."

A red sun was slowly setting, making the dancing shadows of breeze-blown tree branches seem choreographed. Turing to leave, Bryce, with his arm around Traci's waist, whispered in her ear.

She smiled.

CHAPTER FIFTEEN

Winding through the Austrian Alps on the route from Salzburg to Florence is a virtual treasure trove of breathtaking beauty. The train glides smoothly up mountain sides and into valleys, through dark tunnels whose ends are met with a flash of brilliant sunlight beaming from a cloudless azure sky, along ridges looking down upon terraced vineyards and orchards and small villages tucked away on the banks of crystal clear rivers.

In less than three hours the train pulls into the Italian border town of Tarviso, followed by Venice and Bologna. Total travel time Salzburg to Florence is nine hours.

Although distracted many times by the magnificence of the passing landscape, Bryce was able to draft a response to Zach Tillson's email message. When he felt it conveyed what he wanted Tillson to hear, he gave it to Traci for review.

Dear Zach,

Thank you for your kind remarks regarding Lauren's death. It's been a difficult time of adjustment for me, but I'm gaining on it.

Thanks too for the assurance we will be able to work amicably in resolving the dispute between our clients. Although Sister Teresa was undeniably anguished over the unjust and insensitive manner in which she was summarily dismissed from her position by your client, we are willing to consider a meeting with the two of you. If such a meeting occurs, the discussion will be on the record and admissible as testimony should we subsequently file a defamation of character suit against your client.

In that event, one of our pretrial motions will seek a writ of 'duces tecum' to subpoena all of Sister Teresa's personnel files containing letters of commendation, administrative evaluations, peer evaluations and parent/guardian feedback. These files will portray Sister Teresa in her true light: a caring, giving dedicated professional. The onus of proving she is anything less will be squarely upon your client.

I'm hoping in one or more of the lengthy discussions you've had with your client, he's confided in you as to who the bad guy in this whole mess really is. If he hasn't, it's in his – and your – best interest for him to do so.

Sister Teresa wants me to convey her appreciation for the sound advice you gave your client regarding Father Michael.

I'm still unsure when either Sister Teresa or I will be back in the Bay Area; however, I agree with your assessment that the press of time is not a major factor.

Your friend and colleague,

Bryce Gibson

"Great!" Traci said, handing the pad back to Bryce. "I feel a little strange, though, to still be referred to as 'Sister Teresa' when I've made up my mind I'm leaving the order."

"Making up your mind to leave and actually doing it are separate issues. As your lawyer, my advice is to not go public with your intentions to resign until all of this is behind us. It'll be to our advantage, especially if we go to trial, for you to still have the affiliation."

───────────

Before the train pulled into the Florence station Bryce confessed he had fudged a little on his hotel routine and had emailed ahead for reservations before leaving Salzburg. The two-star Rayan Palace Hotel, located just two blocks from the train station, was a favorite of Lauren's because of its location, attractiveness of the rooms, and the friendliness of the couple who own and operate the 12-room hotel.

Immediately after checking in, Bryce and Traci became eager tourists. So much to see, so little time.

The beauty of Florence isn't found on the streets or the exterior of the mostly gray stone buildings. An exception is the Duomo Santa Maria del Fiore, a Gothic cathedral which has long been a symbol of Florence. Begun in 1296 as a deliberate challenge to the great cathedrals then rising in Pisa and Siena, the people of Florence announced their cathedral would be the greatest building in the world.

The first architect, Arnolfo di Cambio, drew a plan and construction work went very well for over 100 years. The building was nearly completed by 1418 – all except for the enormous dome. The dome was designed by Filippo Brunelleschi and utilized a cantilevered system which took another 16 years to complete. As with many Florentine churches, the façade was left unfinished until it was inlaid with striking pink, green, and white Tuscan marble in the late 1800's.

Standing in front of the Duomo watching Traci take picture after picture, Bryce once again was taken by the similarities between Traci and Lauren. He quickly switched his focus remembering her admonition at the train station in Nuremburg, "Keep in mind, while I may be like her, I can never be her."

Florence was ruled almost continuously for over 300 years by the Medici family – from 1434 until the last of the Medici, Anna Maria Lodovica, died in 1743. Two of the most important members of the family were Cosimo, who ruled from 1434 until his death in 1464 and his brilliant grandson Lorenzo who ruled from 1469 until he died in 1492.

Lorenzo assumed leadership of the family and the city at the age of 20. Though he was a physically unattractive man with a very large nose and harsh squeaky voice, he was popular among all classes. He was a gifted statesman, poet, musician and philosopher. He was also capable of recognizing genius in others. One of the many artists he encouraged was the young Michelangelo. His death at the early age of 43 was a tragedy for Florence.

The evening was cool and refreshing as Bryce showed Traci some other landmarks on their zigzag route back to the hotel. Along the way they had pizza and beer, looking on as throngs of pedestrians crowded the sidewalks and hundreds of mopeds dominated the streets, sounding like so many giant bumblebees.

Arriving at the hotel, Traci said a quick goodnight in the hallway and went to her room for a long, hot bubble bath soak. Bryce wanted to suggest they share a bottle of wine before separating for the night but thought better of it as Traci seemed pensive, almost distracted. Bryce sat in an overstuffed easy chair watching the last rays of the Tuscan sun fade into the horizon. For reasons he couldn't get a handle on, he felt a growing concern for Traci. Why was she reluctant to hold his hand as they walked about the city? Why was she quiet at dinner and ate so little when usually she's both talkative and famished? Why didn't she give any indication she would like a goodnight kiss? What is she thinking at this moment?

His mind shifted into a lower gear and began a brief tour of introspection. His 'sentimental journey' was nothing like he expected. Instead of its being a long, possibly sad, trip with Lauren down memory lane as he anticipated, he was actually having one of the best times of his life. While Lauren's presence was felt occasionally, it was no longer constant. It had been days since looking through the picture album; Lauren's journal had stayed in the suitcase. Should he be feeling guilty for feeling so good?

It was almost nine in the morning. When Traci hadn't arrived with her usual door rap, Bryce called her room. No answer. A moment of panic rushed through his body as he moved quickly down the two flights of stairs to the lobby. No one was at the desk; the lobby was empty. Heading for the entry door to search for her on the street, he passed a small breakfast room.

"Bryce," he heard Traci's voice call. "I'm in here having coffee."

He entered the room letting out an audible sigh of relief; his face a paler shade of white. Traci was alone in the room. Bryce was at her table in a heartbeat!

"Oh my goodness, Traci, don't ever do that again," he pleaded. "Please let me know when you plan to go off by yourself."

"I'm sorry," she said apologetically. "I lost track of time. I meant to be in my room an hour ago. I went for a walk to help clear my head and when I got back the coffee aroma lured me in here."

Bryce poured himself a cup of coffee and topped-off Traci's before sitting down. Attempting to make small talk he asked, "Did you have a good night?"

"My night gets mixed reviews," she answered. "I spent most of it doing inventory."

"What kind of inventory?"

"Of our time together. It's pretty amazing. Even though we've known each other for a very short time as the calendar goes, I feel I've known you for years. You have a wonderful transparency about you. You're open and honest about everything – your feelings, your emotions, your past – and yet your ego is strong and your psyche intact."

"That goes for you too, Traci. I've never been more comfortable talking with anyone. Lauren was a good conversationalist and very knowledgeable on a wide variety of topics but it seemed to me she was more at ease sharing thoughts and ideas in group settings than one-on-one."

A hotel staff member came in carrying a basket of freshly baked pastries and put them on the serving counter before smiling and leaving.

"Those look delicious," Traci said, standing and walking toward the counter. "Could I bring you one?"

"Yes, please," Bryce said. "Maybe you should have two. You sure didn't eat much of the pizza last night."

"I know. I wasn't in a very good space most of yesterday."

"I thought something was bothering you, and it seemed to keep growing as the day went on."

"Yes, you're right about that. I needed time to sort it out and test myself before sharing with you."

"So . . . do you have it sorted now?"

"I think so. At least I can give it a try. I've grappled with myself to validate my feelings. I don't want to make a mistake and I don't want to embarrass you."

"I can't imagine you doing or saying anything that would embarrass me," Bryce said convincingly.

"Okay, then, I'll jump in with both feet. Bryce Canyon Gibson, I'm falling in love with you. I've been fighting it from the time we left London. Last night I made up my mind I had to let you know. I enjoy being with you more than I've ever enjoyed being with anyone. Before and during my affair with Kevin, I was sure the feeling I had for him was love. In reality it was merely all-consuming infatuation. What I feel for you when I'm with you, apart from you, or just thinking about you is a love I can literally feel maturing hour by hour, day by day."

Bryce sat basking in the glow of stunned disbelief.

"I realized what was happening was something I needed to get a grip on. When we were in Bruges I stayed behind at the Church of Our Lady for a purpose. I felt I needed to go to confession and let a priest know I was falling in love with a man still in love with his wife, even though his wife was deceased. I'm glad I did that. He gave me some very good advice."

"What was the advice?" Bryce was curious to know, asking the question through a broad smile.

"Have a patient heart, and follow where it leads."

Bryce wanted to say something, or sing something, or shout "alleluia" to the rafters; but Traci put her fingers to his lips, letting him know nothing was expected. The look on his face, in his eyes, told her she had not embarrassed him.

"I have other thoughts I might share as the day goes on, but this is it for now," Traci informed him. "Please don't send the email to Zach Tillson until we've talked some more. Now, let's get ready for the day."

———————

To avoid the long lines that clog the queue to the entrance of the Galleria dell'Accademia, the home of Michelangelo's David, it's wise to arrive before the doors open for the day. Although the museum is filled with Renaissance paintings, it is most famous for two of Michelangelo's masterpieces, David and his unfinished Prisoners. The David is one of the great symbols of the Renaissance which marked the return of man, not God, as the subject of art. Looking like a realistic individual instead of an idealized being, the statue builds on the art of the classical Greeks. The story of David and Goliath had great meaning to the citizens of Florence who saw themselves in David as they overcame the giant neighboring cities of Pisa and Siena. David's large right hand is said to symbolize the hand of God granting power to slay the giant.

In addition to viewing David Bryce had planned a walk from the Academy to the Pitti Palace located across the Arno River to the south. Along the route they would pass by the Baptistery, Florence's oldest building and one of the most imposing Romanesque buildings in Tuscany and Plazzo Vecchio, the palace-home of the Medici.

To cross the river they would use Ponte Vecchio which connects Palazzo Vecchio and the Pitti Palace. This famous bridge is lined with shops that traditionally sold gold and silver exclusively and has been given the common name "Gold Bridge." Today the bridge teems with shops of all types, artist stalls and street musicians. This is the only bridge over the Arno the retreating Nazi forces didn't blow up in their retreat from Florence.

Their last tourist stop for the day would be the Pitti Palace which the Medici used as their country retreat to escape the smells and discomforts of Florence's bustling streets. Today the palace houses several museums. Behind the palace are the Boboli Gardens designed in the 16th century. Inside is the Palatine Gallery with the largest collection of works by Raphael to be found in the world. The Modern Art Gallery houses a collection of 19th and 20th century Tuscan paintings; and the Grand Ducal Treasures which displays, among other valuable relics, a collection of the Medici family jewels.

The walking tour from monument to monument was delightful; window shopping along the way fun and holding hands while making small talk as they strolled, relaxing. But in the mix of all this, Bryce's male curiosity was asking the unspoken question, when is she going to get back to this morning's conversation? It was her agenda to complete, and he knew she would in her own good time.

That time came when Traci asked if they could stop and sit on a rustic bench in the shade of a large olive tree. Before starting to share her thoughts, she kissed Bryce, first on the forehead, then on the cheek.

"The reason I asked you to wait before sending a response to Zach," she began, "was to give me more time to sort through my emotions. In reading what you propose to send, I counted five references to 'Sister Teresa'. I told you then my being identified as 'Sister Teresa' makes me feel strange because I plan to resign from my order and live my life as Traci Dunne. I really appreciate the advice you gave me, as my lawyer, to not leave the order until all the legal rigmarole is out of the way."

"Would you be more comfortable if I changed the reference to 'my client'?" Bryce asked. "It really doesn't matter."

"No, but thanks for the suggestion. I need to remind myself more and more that I'm still 'Sister Teresa' and our fight with Norton is more than his being a pig to a woman – which is disgusting in any case – but his total disrespect for the religion he so hypocritically uses to his advantage."

"I love you, Traci Dunne," Bryce blurted unequivocally. "I honestly love you."

"Oh, Bryce. Are you sure? I mean really, truly sure."

"Yes. I'm sure. I'm totally sure. I know what love is; I know what it feels like and I know how it makes me feel. Lauren taught me how to recognize and accept love for what it is in its deepest sense: a lifetime commitment to share good times and bad."

Traci moved as close to Bryce as she could. He put his arm around her shoulder and held her tightly.

"There's one other thing to talk about," Traci said. "When I became a Sister in my order, I took certain vows. These vows were considered to be promises to God and weren't to be taken lightly or applied subjectively to adjust to different situations."

Bryce relaxed his hold on Traci, allowing her to shift so she could look at him.

"One of the most important vows I took was the vow of celibacy," Traci said in a serious tone. "You need to know I intend to keep that vow until I officially resign, and beyond. On my wedding night, whenever that may be and with whomever I marry, I will be released from the vow, but not a day sooner."

"Some things in life are well worth waiting for," Bryce said. "I think I can answer your question now."

"What question?" Traci wanted to know.

"My beliefs about Heaven and hell."

"That was a while back. I thought maybe you'd forgotten."

"No, I hadn't. I just needed to find the right context for an answer that made sense to me. Now I have one. I believe there are some people who are born basically good, and some bad. We all live our lives with the opportunity to become better. These are personal choices, and no one can make them for us. Those who come into the world good, and choose to become better, make the world a better place for everyone else. Those who come in bad, and refuse to become better, make the world worse for everyone else.

"And then we die," Bryce said without changing his expression.

"Those who chose to make life better go to a place, for want of a better term, we call 'Heaven'; those who refuse to become better go to 'hell.' A few – those who were exceptionally good – get to return and have a 'Heaven on Earth' experience. I must have been one of those in my last life because I'm sure this is Heaven."

"You're quite the theologian," Traci laughed. "But don't give up your day job."

CHAPTER SIXTEEN

THREE days after they shared thoughts on love and life, Bryce and Traci were on a train taking them to the Provence region of southern France. They concluded those days in Tuscany were the best of the trip and attributed the reason to the relief of internal tensions which had been building over several weeks.

Bryce wanted Traci to see a softer side of Tuscany so the morning after professing their mutual love they boarded a local bus taking them to the hill village of San Gimignano, an hour southwest of Florence. The little town is commonly referred to as "the city of the beautiful towers" as there were once more than 70 towers, of which 13 survive today. Each tower belonged to a family or corporation, desperately striving to rise above their neighbors so they could better defend themselves during times of raids by dropping pitch or burning oil on their enemies.

From San Gimignano another bus took them to Siena, a city of opposites from Florence. Where Florentine buildings are classically inspired and built of brown or grey stone, Siena's are Gothic and built of reddish-brown brick, the color known to artists as burnt sienna. Where Florence is dour and masculine, Siena is graceful and feminine. Looking at today's population differences of 500,000 for Florence and 60,000 for Siena, it's hard to realize that during the Middle Ages the two cities fought battles on equal footing. Gradually, however, the sheer power and wealth of Florence, combined with its political clout wore down its rival.

Bryce and Traci had toyed with the idea of cutting the 'sentimental journey' short since both were now somewhat eager to return home. The compromised decision was to continue on to Provence for a few days then visit Barcelona. From there they would go directly to Paris, then back to London. The only significant change in the itinerary was to eliminate the Basque Country segment.

From the four Provence towns Bryce offered as possibilities for staying, Traci chose Arles, the old stomping grounds of Vincent Van Gough. The train route between Florence and Arles would take them through Pisa, Genoa, Monaco, Nice and Marseilles.

In Monaco the train had a scheduled 40 minute wait, enough time for Traci to run to the front of the station and take pictures of the palace, perched on a high precipice overlooking the Mediterranean Sea. She added Monaco to her collection of countries.

While it would mean arriving in Arles late in the day, Bryce suggested they spend a couple of hours in Nice, the start of the French Riviera. Traci enthusiastically agreed. After placing their luggage in a storage locker they walked hand-in-hand down the broad esplanade leading to the beach. Once there, two things surprised Traci: the cobbled beach has no sand and most of the women have no tops to their swim suits.

The Rhone River winds its way through the heart of Arles as it forms the Camargue delta. Arles was established by the Greeks in 6th century BC under the name of Theline. Captured by the Celtics in 535 BC, it was renamed Arelate. The Romans took the town in 123 BC and developed it into an important city, building a canal link to the Mediterranean in 104 BC. However, it struggled to get from under the shadow of Marseilles further along the coast.

Arelate's opportunity came when it joined forces with Julius Caesar against Pompey, providing military support. Marseilles backed Pompey and when Caesar defeated Pompey, Marseilles was stripped of its possessions and given to Arelate as a reward. Roman Arelate covered an area of almost 100 acres and possessed a wide array of monuments, including an amphitheater, triumphal arch, Roman circus, theater and a full circuit of walls.

The city reached a peak of influence during the 4th and 5th centuries AD when it was used as headquarters for Roman Emperors engaged in military campaigns. In 395 it became the seat of the Praetorian Prefecture of the Gauls, governing the western part of the Western Empire which included Gaul proper plus Spain and Brittany.

It became a favorite city of Constantine I who built baths there, substantial remains of which are still standing. His son, Constantine II, was born there. When the usurper to the throne, Constantine III declared himself emperor in the West, he renamed the city Arles in 408.

Medieval Arles was badly affected by the invasion of Provence by the Muslim Saracens and the Franks who took control of the region in the 8th century. Over the next four centuries the Kingdom of Arles was a pawn to such players as the Saracens and Viking raiders; Rodolphe, Count of Auxerre; Hugh of Arles gave his kingdom up to Rodolphe II; when Rodolphe III died the Kingdom was inherited by Emperor Conrad II the Salic.

Most of the territory of the kingdom was progressively incorporated into France. The town regained its political and economical prominence in the 12th century, with the Holy Roman Emperor Frederick Barbarossa going there in 1178 for his coronation. Also, in the 12th century it became a free city governed by an elected magistrate. The city retained this status until the French Revolution of 1789.

Arles remained economically important for many years as a major port on the Rhone. The arrival of the railway in the 19th century eventually eliminated much of the river trade, leading to the town becoming something of a backwater.

On the positive side, this made the town an attractive destination for the painter Vincent Van Gogh, who arrived there in February, 1888. He was fascinated by the Provencal landscapes, producing over 300 paintings and drawings during his time in Arles, including Café Terrace at Night, Yellow House, Starry Night Over the Rhone, L'Arlesienne and Room at Arles. When van Gogh's health deteriorated causing him to become alarmingly eccentric, culminating in the infamous ear-severing incident in December 1888, concerned citizens circulated a petition demanding he be confined. In May 1889 van Gogh left Arles and was admitted to the asylum in nearby Saint-Remy.

Arriving at the Arles railroad station at dusk, Bryce quickly phoned the Hotel le Cloitre to check on room availability. Once again he was successful making reservations. The Cloitre is a renovated monastery, a hidden jewel down a winding road between the ancient Roman Theater and Place de la Republic, one of the city's 'happening' spots.

The evening was balmy and, if the day on the train hadn't been so long, the intrepid travelers might have ventured out for the evening but opted instead to sit in the hotel's small patio area, sipping Chianti and listening to the cooing of doves as they settled into their roosts for the night.

"What a perfect night," Bryce said, breaking the silence. "Paris aside, of all the places in Europe I've been, I love Provence the most. The countryside, the villages, the history, the culture, the people. I love everything about it. If we had more time we would rent a car and explore the whole region: drive to small hilltop hamlets, walk through fields of lavender, splurge at street markets, stand in front of the house where Nostradamus was born, explore the chateau fortress at Les Baux, taste wine at Chateauneuf-du Pape, go to a concert in the antique amphitheater in Orange, tour the Palace of the Popes in Avignon, ride carousels. . ."

"Whoa, steady there, amigo," Traci laughed. "If you want to do those things, let's do them. I'm really intrigued."

"Someday we will," Bryce assured her, "when our work at home is out of the way."

Two full days in Arles proved to be all Bryce could hope for during their limited stay. His planned tour started by going to many of the large outdoor landmarks, following the Van Gogh trail and spending time in the Saturday market.

The most obvious structure in the city is the Roman Arena where, 2000 years ago, gladiators fought wild animals to the screaming delight of 20,000 fans. Today it's the home of concerts and an occasional bull fight. Until the early 1800's this stadium corralled 200 small homes and functioned as a town within a town.

Very near the Hotel le Cloitre are remains of the Theatre Antique. Built in the first century BC it had a seating capacity of 10,000 and was the venue for dramatic productions – the Arlesians were very much into comedy, very little into tragedy. Although there is a chain-link fence surrounding the paid-audience area and stage, musical events are easily observed from the sidewalk – and heard for blocks away.

Another interesting landmark, which brings together antiquity and modern day, is Place du Forum, the political and religious center of Roman Arles. Named for the Roman Forum that once stood here, this café-crammed square is one of the liveliest spots in town. In close proximity is the Cryptoportiques du Forum, the only Baroque church in Arles. In addition to its wood ceilings, it provides a dramatic entry to an underground system of arches and vaults supporting the southern end of the Roman Forum and provided a hiding place for resistance fighters during World War II.

One of the major cornerstones of the Place de la Republic is St. Trophime Cloisters and Church, named for a third century bishop of Arles. The church boasts the finest Romanesque doorway to be found anywhere. The semicircular tympanum above the door is filled with Christian symbolism: Christ sits in majesty, surrounded by symbols of four disciples. Matthew is the winged man; Mark, the winged lion; Luke, the ox; and John, the eagle.

Street markets are both prominent and popular throughout most of Europe and none are more so than those in Provence. The Arles market – available on Wednesday and Saturday – are set up just outside the north wall of the city and stretch for a dozen blocks from the old city gate eastward. Where nothing is found except residential streets on Tuesday and Friday nights, by morning of the next days, those same streets are bustling with commerce. Almost everything imaginable is available to buy. If you're looking for fresh fruit and vegetables, cheese, raw or cooked beef, chicken, pork, rabbit or quail; a dozen varieties of olives; clothing, baskets of all sizes and shapes; works of art; leather goods; jewelry; pottery; and scores of other items, they are to be found in the market.

Then, as magically as the market appears, it disappears within an hour after closing time.

Traci's first purchase was a medium-sized floppy straw basket with leather handles. "When the basket is full," she told Bryce, "I'll be ready to leave."

CHAPTER SEVENTEEN

TWO hundred miles and a world of cultural differences separate Arles from Barcelona. It's an easy trip with only two train changes. The first is in Avignon, the major transfer station for passengers wanting to head west rather than staying on the northbound run to Lyon or Paris. The other transfer point is on the border between France and Spain at Cerbere.

Regardless of the port of entry between France and Spain, a train change is required. This is due to the misfortune of a major decision, taken at an early stage in the development of the Spanish rail system to place the rails on an unusually broad gauge track. Some believe the choice of gauge was influenced by Spain's hostility to France in the 1850s, thinking that making the railway network incompatible with that of France would hinder any French invasion. Other sources state the decision was made to allow bigger engines with more power to climb Spain's steep mountain passes.

"As eager as I am to get home and start the ball rolling at the courthouse," Bryce said as the Spanish train moved swiftly south, "I'm glad we're going to Barcelona. The places we've been are all special for their own reasons, but compared to Barcelona they're very sedate. Barcelona is a party town, waking up after the sun sets and staying awake until the sun rises."

"Does this mean we can go dancing again?" Traci asked hopefully.

"You bet. Dance halls are everywhere but we won't have to look for one. In Barcelona, there's dancing in the streets."

———————

The heartbeat of Barcelona is along the broad boulevard La Rambla with its upper end at Placa Cataluña and lower end below the monument to Christopher Columbus. In between, and all along the way, this unique street is a cacophony of sound and a rainbow of color.

Until the beginning of the 18th century, La Rambla was just a path beside a stream running between convents on one side and the old city wall on the other. In 1704 the first houses were built at the Boqueria on the site of the old city wall and the first trees were planted. In 1775, the city walls by the Drassanes medieval shipyards were demolished, and toward the end of the 18th century as the street began to be systematically developed, La Rambla became a tree-lined avenue.

Gradually, over the decades that followed, the street began to flourish with commerce; it became the principal meeting place for conversation and recreation. The 20 minute easy stroll from top to bottom starts with the wealthy section and ends on the rough Mediterranean port dock. Along the way a mixture of Barcelonan life is experienced: the opera house; elegant cafes, artists, street mimes; musicians; and here and there a roof top or balcony obviously a Gaudi design.

For those who want to stop and enter buildings, or simply people-watch, there are ample opportunities. The Academy of Science and the Baroque church have much to offer, as does La Boqueria Market with a large selection of fruits and vegetables, broiled chickens, bags of live snails, full legs of ham and 25 kinds of olives. Further down, the Placa Reial holds its own fascination with old-fashioned taverns, modern bars featuring patio seating and the artist Antoni Gaudi's first public works – two colorful helmeted lampposts. Just back across the Ramblas, Palau Guell offers an enjoyable look at a Gaudi interior.

The bottom of the Ramblas is marked by the Columbus Monument, a 197-foot-tall structure built for an 1888 exposition. Some find it interesting that Barcelona would honor a man whose discoveries of the new world ultimately led to the demise of the city's great trading power. It was at this place in Barcelona where Ferdinand and Isabel welcomed Columbus home from his first voyage to America.

After they walked the length of the Ramblas, Bryce suggested they go back a couple of blocks to a sidewalk café they passed that wasn't overly crowded to have a late lunch and a pitcher of sangria – a refreshing drink concocted from wine, brandy, sugar, orange juice and soda water.

"Having fun?" Bryce asked when they were seated.

"So much," Traci answered. "I always had a different picture in my mind as to what Spain is like."

"I know. This part of the country is really different from the rest; not only the landscape, but the people and culture as well. We're actually in Catalonia, an Autonomous Community which corresponds to most of the territory of the former Principality of Catalonia. Barcelona's its capital and the more than 7,000,000 people who live in the region consider themselves to be Catalonian rather than Spanish. Even so, the Spanish constitution declares Spain to be an indissoluble nation that recognizes and guarantees the right of Catalonia to self-govern."

"Thanks so much for clearing that up," Traci laughed. "I'm a little confused, though, about my country collection."

"Let's talk about our time here," Bryce suggested. There's so much to do and see but I think we should leave for Paris no later than day after tomorrow. I want to show you two places, at least. One is the Picasso Museum and the other, Gaudi's Unfinished Cathedral. We can walk to the museum this afternoon. Tonight we can kick back and have fun eating, people-watching and dancing – which means we'll be sleeping late in the morning. Tomorrow we'll go to the Cathedral."

"Sounds perfect," Traci said quickly.

Pablo Picasso was born in 1881 and died in 1973. He lived in Barcelona from age 14 to 21 so the best collection of his early works anywhere is found in the Picasso Museum. Picasso's personal secretary put together a large collection of his works and donated it to the city. The collection is presented in 12 stages of Picasso's life.

Stage One is dubbed "Boy Wonder" and exhibits the genius of his talent at ages 12-14. Stage Two is his work from 'Malaga' where he first dabbles in Impressionism, unknown in Spain at the time. Stage Three, or 'Sponge' phase, is his effort as a 15-year-old to dutifully enter art-school competitions. Winning the second place prize for his entry Science and Charity, Picasso got the chance to study in Madrid.

Stage Four is called 'Independence'. In 1898 he visits Horta, a rural Catalan village and discovers his artistic independence. Stage Five is 'Sadness' to depict the death of his good friend. He returns to Barcelona in 1899 and finds Art Nouveau the rage. He quits art school and hangs out with the avant-garde crowd – much to the distress of his father. During this stage, Picasso continues to exert his artistic independence by painting portraits of his friends. Although he is still a teenager, Picasso puts on his first one-man show.

Stage Six is 'Paris, 1900-1901'. Picasso, at age 19, arrives in Paris and lets his prolific and eclectic talent have its head. He goes Bohemian and consorts with poets, prostitutes and artists. He paints Impressionist landscapes akin to Monet; posters like Toulouse-Lautrec; and still-lifes imitating Cezanne. It was Cezanne's technique of 'building' a figure with 'cubes' of paint that led Picasso to invent Cubism.

Stage Seven was Picasso's 'Blue Period, 1901-1904' brought on by the bleak Paris winters and his state of poverty. To stay housed and fed, he cranked out scores of painting in blue – the coldest color. This concept, although not intentional on his part, was revolutionary in art history. Now the artist is painting not what he sees but what he feels. Fortunately, Stage Eight, 'Rose' shows a woman in pink, painted with classic 'Spanish melancholy' which pulls him out of the doldrums.

Stage Nine was Picasso's 'Cubism, 1907-1920' era. Picasso invented the shocking Cubist genre in Paris. The Museum has no true Cubist paintings but the art form is discussed in detail. Stage Ten depicts the 'Eclectic, 1920-1950' in which he paints individuals to look like sturdy statues; symbolism where a bullfighter's horse becomes the innocent victim and the bull the killing tyrant. Picasso mixed symbols masterfully in his painting Geurnica to show the horror of war.

Stage Eleven, 'Picasso and Velazquez, 1957' shows the playful sides of these two Spanish geniuses. Picasso had great respect for Velazquez and painted over 50 interpretations of Velazquez's Las Meninas, the creation many critics consider to be the best painting by anyone ever. In the Stage Eleven rooms, it's fun to see all of the ways Picasso filtered Velazquez's masterpiece of realism through the kaleidoscope of Cubism.

Finally, in Stage Twelve 'Windows, 1957', Picasso gives visual meaning to his mantra, "Paintings are like windows open to the world." Here is the French Riviera. Radiant with simple black outlines and pastel colors in crayon, this canvas beams with sun-splashed nature and the joys of the beach.

Picasso died without ever seeing the Barcelona Museum that bears his name. As an outspoken opponent of Ferdinand Franco's fascist dictatorship, Picasso vowed to never return to Spain while Franco remained in power. Picasso died in 1973; Franco in 1975.

As Bryce had promised, the night out in Barcelona was magical. After the Picasso Museum tour, they went to their hotel rooms to rest up for the evening. They ventured onto the Rambla a little before ten.

The problem for couples after dark in Barcelona is trying to choose what to do from all that's offered. Bryce and Traci started their night with an authentic dinner in a classy restaurant. Also as Bryce had promised, there was dancing in the street to music provided by a number of groups. They opted instead to spend an hour in a discotheque before moving to a flamenco dance hall. Their gala time ended with visiting a music club to relax listening to jazz and blues.

They were blissfully fatigued when they returned to the hotel. As always, Bryce accompanied Traci to her room. She invited him in. They stood, looking into each other's eyes with growing emotion. Bryce took Traci in his arms and enjoyed her body pressing against his. He kissed her passionately, tasting the sweetness of her lips. She returned his embrace, and his kiss.

"I love you Traci," he said softly. "Those healing hands of time have done their job."

"And I love you, my darling Bryce," she whispered in his ear.

"Sleep as long as you like, and have pleasant dreams," Bryce said, leaving the room. "Let me know when you're awake."

Bryce's sleep habits never permitted him to sleep past seven in the morning regardless of his bedtime. Remembering there was an overnight sleeper train from Barcelona to Paris, he wrote a note to Traci and slid it under her door saying he had gone to the train station to check on the schedule. His memory served him well. The train would leave Barcelona at 9:05 in the evening and arrive in Paris at nine the next morning. He made reservations for two single-occupancy sleeper units, pleased with knowing they would have more time in Paris.

One of the most enduring worldwide symbols of Barcelona is Antoni Gaudi's La Sagrada Famila or as it's more commonly known, "The Unfinished Cathedral." This is arguably Gaudi's greatest masterpiece, and one Bryce was eager for Traci to visit before they left for Paris.

Gaudi was an architect and artist born in 1852 and, because of the modernistic feel in much of his work he is seen by some as being a man before his time. He had an uncanny ability to see forms directly in space without needing plans; although he drew precise plans for the builders to follow. Gaudi began construction of La Sagrada Famila in 1883 and lived on the site for more than a decade before his untimely death – he was run over and killed by a streetcar – in 1926. By the time of his death he had devoted 43 years of his life to the project.

He is buried in the cathedral's crypt and from the museum, located in the basement, a window allows visitors to look down and view his tomb. Since his death, construction has continued in fits and starts and isn't expected to be finished for another 50 years. The only construction money available is from donations and entrance fees. When the cathedral is completed, a dozen 140 foot tall spires – representing the apostles – will stand in groups of four and mark the three entry facades if the building. The center tower, honoring Jesus, will reach 560 feet and be flanked by 400 foot towers of Mary and the four evangelists.

The towers are like no other church or cathedral in the world. They have to be seen to be believed as they are comically beautiful – indescribable in color and design – almost organic in feeling.

"What an amazing man and what a wonderful piece of art," Traci said as they stood for one final look before walking back to the hotel. "It's so sad he didn't live longer to see more of it completed."

"We'll have to come back from time to time and check on its progress," Bryce suggested. "If we return every ten years, we can look forward to being in Barcelona at least five more times."

CHAPTER EIGHTEEN

BRYCE was filled with buoyant anticipation as he lay in his narrow bed watching lights of small towns flash like fireflies through the small window of his sleeper. So much had changed since he first planned this trip, this "Sentimental Journey." What started out to be a journey of sad reminiscing had become one of unexpected joy; loneliness had been replaced with love; gloom had been extinguished by a rushing river of glee.

He and Traci sat in the train's café car for the first hour after leaving Barcelona, sipping wine, talking about the near-term future and making a list of Traci's "must see" activity priorities for Paris. For her, Paris – to be Paris – had to include, the Eiffel Tower, the Arc de Triomphe, Notre Dame and the Louvre. Bryce placed these on the list, drew a circle and labeled those sites "Day One." They parted for the night agreeing to meet for breakfast an hour before reaching Paris.

Wondering what might be happening at home relating to Bishop Grogan and Clifton Norton tried to get some of Bryce's thought time, but he overrode any intrusion by forming his "what I want Traci to see" list in his head. This proved to be no simple task. He and Lauren had visited Paris more than a dozen times and with each trip they discovered something new. Without turning on the light or finding his list, he made mental notes of the possibilities.

They would be staying at the Hotel Odessa on the Left Bank's Montparnasse District, just a few blocks from the Montparnasse train station. The Odessa was the one important reservation Bryce made before starting the trip. To him, this part of the city was the true Paris and he considered the Odessa to be his Paris home. Also, the location provides a good launch pad for heading in any direction. The Edgar Quinet Metro subway stop is just across the street. He had called the Odessa the afternoon of their leaving Barcelona to reconfirm his reservation and to add a second room.

Hitting Traci's monuments on the first day would be doable, except for the Louvre which – to do it justice – should be given a half-day in itself. After settling into the hotel they could go immediately to the Eiffel Tower, just 15 minutes away on Metro. From there they could stroll along the bank of the Seine to Pont de l'Alma and see the underpass where Princess Diana's tragic death occurred. A footbridge connecting to the Right Bank crosses the Seine at this point and one metro stop away finds the Arc de Triomphe standing majestically at the west end of Paris' grand avenue, the Champs Elyesse.

Those who care to climb the spiral stairway to the top of the Arc get a great view not only of that part of Paris but also have a bird's-eye look at the world's best traffic circle, where 12 vehicle-packed avenues converge.

Bryce realized just before dropping to sleep he would need Traci's input before setting a firm Paris itinerary. If she wanted more museum time in addition to the Louvre, he would recommend Musee d'Orsay which houses French art from the 1800's; the small but impressive Orangerie in the Tuileries Garden immediately west of the Louvre; or visiting Napoleon's Tomb in the magnificent Les Invalides.

Notre Dame Cathedral could be supplemented by Sainte-Chappell – a Gothic masterpiece of glass construction – and the Byzantine Sacre-Coeur church in the Montmartre district perched atop Paris' highest hill. Although it would require a day-trip, the cathedral at Chartres might interest Traci.

Other day-trips to consider are Giverny – the long-time residence of Claude Monet – and the palace at Versailles. For shopping, they couldn't be in a better city than the one in which department stores were invented. Traci could pick from one of four great world-class stores – Printemps, Galeries Lafayette, Bon Marché or Samaritaine. In addition to these department stores, the Forum des Halles is a huge subterranean shopping center.

Paris is a stroller's mecca. Walks along the Seine, stopping to browse through the legendary book stalls lining the north side of Quai St. Michel just west of Notre Dame; Parc Monceau; the grounds surrounding the Grand Palais; and Parc du Champ de Mars provide beautiful and relaxing environments. Within easy walking distance of the Odessa Hotel are the Luxembourg Gardens and the historic Montparnasse Cemetery which provides the final resting place for poets, artists, and politicians.

Bryce was starting his second cup of coffee when Traci arrived for breakfast, promptly on time. She looked well-rested and beautiful, ready to take Paris by storm. While waiting, Bryce had written his schedule thoughts on a legal pad and arranged the possibilities of things to do and places to see into separate columns.

"Here's your Chinese menu," he said, sliding the pad in front of Traci. "Pick as many items as you like and we'll go through all we have time for."

Traci asked many questions about a number of possibilities and noticed – to Bryce's chagrin – the Opera House wasn't on the list. "I've been to Phantom of the Opera three times and I would really like being in the building and seeing the authentic chandelier."

By the time the train pulled into the Montparnasse station they had honed the list to a sharp focus, creating a workable plan that could be accommodated within an eight day timeframe.

Leaving the train station and standing for a few minutes to watch and listen to the music of a large carousel, Bryce couldn't stop grinning like a schoolboy, nor did he want to. He inhaled large breaths of air and let them out slowly. Crossing the street and walking toward the hotel, he pointed out his favorite boulangerie ("the best croissants in the world are baked right here"); a large multipurpose Monoprix store ("the entire lower level is bulging with great takeout deli food and wines from all over France"); a small, intimate Italian restaurant ("we'll come here for their great spaghetti marinara").

The lobby of the Odessa is short and narrow but inviting, with dark polished wood, shining brass fittings, eye-catching spiral stairs with wrought iron railings and red carpet stairs. The desk clerk has an unobstructed view of the front door. As Bryce led the way into the building he was greeted by a friendly and welcoming voice.

"Bonjour, Monsieur Gibson. Welcome back. It has been much too long." He smiled and nodded a welcome to Traci.

"Merci beaucoup, Andre. It's good to be back."

"Here are the keys to your rooms. Floor six, as you asked."

As Bryce was showing Traci the small three-person elevator, Andre called to Bryce. "There is this message for you." He handed Bryce a slip of paper. Sharon had called two times in the last three days.

Her message was short and to the point. Important you check email.

They were in adjoining, but not connected rooms. Each had a full bath and large glass double doors opening onto a small balcony overlooking a crossroad of streets already bustling with the day's activity. Since the Odessa had yet to provide internet access for guests, Bryce suggested that while Traci settled in he would go down the block to an Internet Café and see what the commotion was back home.

"What do you think it might be?" Traci asked.

"Don't know, Sweetheart, but Sharon wouldn't be bothering me unless it's a situation that only I can handle. I won't be gone long. We can be at the Eiffel Tower by lunchtime."

Traci was glad for the free time before the day got going. While she did her best on the train to freshen up by using a complete packet of Wet Wipes before meeting Bryce for breakfast, she felt the need for a good long shower.

It was close to an hour later when Bryce returned and knocked on her door. Opening the door to let him in, Traci knew immediately the news was not good. He seemed angry and perplexed, his jaw set firm.

"What, Bryce?" she asked. "What is it?"

He handed Traci the email printout and slumped into a chair. Traci sat on the bed to read.

The letter was from Zach Tillson.

Dear Bryce,

I'm appealing to you as a colleague and, hopefully, a friend. I don't know where you are or what you might be doing to keep you away from SF and out of your office for so long. And, of course, it's none of my business. I've made a real pest of myself with your office over the last week and I'm sure you'll hear from your assistant, Sharon, affirming that fact. She did promise to make an effort to contact you to make sure you know this email is trying to find you.

In paying due diligence to my client Bishop Grogan, I'm duty bound to serve him to the best of my ability. The old man is under so much stress regarding what might happen if you file a suit on behalf of Sister Teresa, his health is being jeopardized. Six days ago he suffered a mild stroke which his doctors say is pressure related. While his prognosis is good, he remains hospitalized so he can be monitored.

So, my appeal to you is based on humanitarian principals. Please get back to the City as soon as you can expedite your return.

With kind regards,

Zach Tillson

Traci bit her lower lip and looked at Bryce for his answer.

"We have to go back right away," he finally admitted. "I thought this through as lucidly as I could before deciding. If Grogan dies before we can start the legal engine, he wins and takes his lies about you to the grave without making amends. Conversely, if he wins by dying, Clifton Norton also wins because Grogan is the key to our complaint against Norton."

"When do we have to leave?" Traci asked. "Can we see a little of Paris at least?"

Bryce moved to Traci and held her. "Yes. It'll take some time to make the flight arrangements. So today we'll go to the Eiffel Tower, the Arc d' Triomphe and Norte Dame. In the morning, I'll take you to the Louvre. While you're enjoying that great place, I'll go to the United Airlines office to get us on a flight from Heathrow to San Francisco and get reservations for London on the Eurostar."

"Would you get the reservations for day after tomorrow?" Traci asked. "Could we have one more night here before leaving?"

"You bet! And we'll make it a night to remember."

CHAPTER NINETEEN

BRYCE worked overtime keeping his frustration in check as he improvised to make optimal use of their abbreviated time in Paris. His plan to have lunch in the Eiffel Tower was scrubbed due to the length of the waiting line for the elevator. Traci took dozens of pictures. What was to be a leisurely-paced walk on the Champs Elyesse to reach the Arc d' Triomphe morphed into a quick-step dash that slowed only to duck into McDonald's for chicken breast sandwiches and a bathroom stop.

By the time they reached Notre Dame the pace of the day was taking its toll. Nearing the cathedral's massive entry doors, they saw a line of people slowly moving through. To their delight and surprise, an organ recital was about to begin. Another serendipitous moment, orchestrated by their guardian angels, designed to provide an hour of spirit-lifting inspiration and personal reflection. At the end of the recital they were relaxed and better able to face the reality of going home.

Before retiring for the evening they sat on the small balcony outside Traci's room. The street below was alive with music and laughter coming from the La Liberte brasserie on the corner opposite the Odessa. The bar's large, brilliant red and green neon sign was one of the many reasons Bryce had for thinking this part of the city represented, to him, the "real Paris."

———————

The Louvre opens its doors at nine thirty each morning, with admission tickets made available a half-hour before. They would be ready to hit the road at eight, have petite dejeuner at the Odessa's sidewalk café and take the Metro to Place d' Concorde – a half-mile from the Louvre – in order to see and appreciate the enormity of the building, parts of which date to the 12th century when it was constructed to be a fortress. Later evolutions saw it used as the royal treasury and as the royal palace.

Once Traci had her admission ticket in hand, along with a map of the interior of the museum, Bryce would don his travel agent hat and make arrangements for their departure the next day. "When I get back, I'll follow the numbered map route until I find you. Have fun, Sweetheart."

Traci was so taken with all the Louvre had to offer she was surprised to find Bryce had been gone for almost five hours before he reappeared.

"Hi, stranger," Traci smiled. "How did you do?"

"Hi, yourself. We're all set. The Eurostar leaves at nine-ten in the morning for London. Our flight from Heathrow isn't until six, so we'll have plenty of time."

They spent another two hours before leaving the Louvre. Traci wanted to go back and see if the crowd around the "Mona Lisa" had thinned out; she needed a closer look. When they did leave, they were greeted by a bath of bright sunlight. They stood for a moment, caught up in the beauty of a vista capturing the Tuileries, the Egyptian obelisk of the Place d' Concorde with the point of its pyramid top centered squarely, like a puzzle piece, into the Arc d' Triomphe miles away. Within the tapestry, the dome of the Invalides and the top third of the Eiffel Tower complete the panorama.

The spell was broken by a gurgling coming from Bryce's stomach.

"Oh, my!" Traci laughed. "Pooh Bear, do I hear a 'rumbly in your tumbly'?"

"I'm afraid so," Bryce answered, pushing on his midsection. "Breakfast was a long time ago."

"It's almost dinner time," Traci suggested. "Why don't we eat something?"

"Great idea. There's a nice little restaurant on Ile Saint-Louis I'd like for us to try. It's a local favorite, just a short distance from Notre Dame. After dinner we can say goodbye to the cathedral and take an evening stroll along the Seine."

The dinner was elegant.

When they arrived at Notre Dame, very few visitors were inside. Without saying a word, Traci went to the altar, knelt down and bowed her head. Bryce slipped into the pew just behind and watched as she meditated. After a few minutes, Bryce stood and moved to the altar. He knelt beside Traci, took her hand in his and lowered his head. For only the fourth time in his adult life,

Bryce Gibson prayed.

By the time they reached the Seine, lights along the lower walkway were reflecting their beams on the rippling water. The night lights of the Eiffel Tower glowed in the distance as the full moon highlighted the golden Pegasus horses on the Alexandre III Bridge. A moonlight-cruising Batabus plowed against the current, sending wavelets splashing against the stone revetment walls.

When an ancient carved wooden bench became available they stopped and sat, looking transfixed at the sights and listening to the seductive sounds of Paris by night. Bryce put his arm around Traci's shoulder and pulled her close. She responded by turning his face toward hers and kissing him in a way that told him he was deeply loved.

Then, in one smooth motion, Bryce pulled a small box from his pocket and knelt on one knee in front of Traci. He showed her the box before opening it. Its texture was black velvet. A one-word logo was on the lid in gold script: Cartier.

Bryce slowly opened the box, revealing a two-carat diamond solitair.

"Teresa Roisin Alana Caitlin Irene Dunne, will you marry me?"

Traci gazed at the lights dancing on the water and reflecting in her eyes.

"Yes, Bryce Canyon Gibson, I will be honored to be your wife."

———————————

The trip from Paris to London was a clockwork event; the jaunt from the Eurostar station to Heathrow on the Tube was equally efficient. After checking in and clearing security they wandered through the myriad of shops looking for keepsakes and gifts. For certain, Bryce needed something very nice for Sharon.

The 'sentimental journey' had gone full circle and as they reminisced, both marveled at the unlikely miracle of their meeting. Traci expressed one very minor concern as she looked at her beautiful ring.

"Do you think people will question how all of this could happen in such a short time?"

"If anyone is concerned, although I can't imagine who that would be, I've calculated the answer. We've been traveling for 42 days. During each of those days we've spent an average of ten constant hours together. This equals 420 waking hours. Assume a typical date on a weekend night lasts five hours. This being the case, we have an equivalency of being on 84 dates. If we went out once a week under normal conditions, by this time we would have been dating for almost a year and a half."

"Will you ever cease to amaze me?" Traci asked.

"Probably. But I hope not for a while."

An hour later they were comfortable in their first-class seats wondering if this plane was the exact one they had flown in when they met. As the giant aircraft thundered down the runway toward takeoff speed Bryce asked, "Where's your rosary?"

"Don't need it," Traci answered, squeezing Bryce's arm. "I have something better."

EPILOGUE

Two weeks after returning from London, Bryce had the first of three meetings with Zach Tillson. In the first meeting Bryce reiterated his plan to file a defamation of character suit against Bishop Grogan. The complaint would not include either the diocese or the school as parties to the suit. Bryce gave Tillson a witness list of a dozen individuals who would testify Grogan had informed them Sister Teresa Dunne was an immoral person who should not be teaching children.

The outcome of the second meeting was a negotiated agreement in which Grogan, under sworn testimony, would reveal Clifton Norton as the source of information which caused Grogan to brand Sister Teresa as immoral.

The third meeting made it incumbent upon the Bishop to send a letter of apology – drafted jointly by Bryce and Zach Tillson – to Sister Teresa, a copy of which would be mailed to each member of the diocese and to all parents and guardians of children enrolled in the diocese school. Once Grogan's testimony was on the record, and the letter sent, the suit against him would be dropped.

Dealing with Clifton Norton, the perpetrator of the slander, proved to be more difficult. His first response when informed by his cadre of lawyers that a potential defamation suit was likely to happen, was to shout in his typical arrogant manner, "Bring 'em on!" Bryce warned that should a suit be filed, he would call a news conference to spell out the bill of particulars. Norton remained defiant.

A week after the filing was recorded, Bryce, as promised, held a news conference on the steps of the courthouse in which he revealed Sister Teresa's rationale for bringing suit. Three weeks later a judge was assigned and a trial date set. Bryce met with Norton's lead attorney and presented him with names of witnesses the plaintiff would be calling to offer testimony. The following day, Norton's lawyer called Bryce for an urgent meeting to discuss an out-of- court settlement.

The witness list included, in addition to Bishop Grogan, the names of four women, all former employees of Norton Industries who – as the result of the news conference – had contacted Bryce and were not just willing, but eager to tell their own stories of Norton's abuse. Norton, after some haggling, offered to pay an undisclosed settlement to Sister Teresa and the four former employees in exchange for their signed and sealed agreement not to bring any future law suits against Norton.

Immediately after the settlement was finalized, Sister Teresa Dunn formally resigned from the religious order that had been the major part of her life for 12 years.

During the course of these events, Bryce and Traci spent as much time together as possible, planning their wedding. A special visiting prelate was flown in to perform the ceremony: Father Michael Dunne, Auxiliary Bishop of the Trenton, New Jersey diocese. It was a small, elegant ceremony in a small, elegant chapel with a dinner reception at the Tiburon Yacht Club. Irish music performed by an accordionist and fiddle player provided the entertainment.

From Tiburon the newlyweds were whisked by limousine to San Francisco International to board a redeye honeymoon flight to Paris. Once airborne, Traci gave Bryce his wedding gift – a leatherbound journal of their travel adventures titled Finding Love in all the Right Places.

Traci, wanting to stay involved in working with and nurturing the lives of children, used the Norton settlement money to incorporate and give direction to the Lauren Fielder Gibson Charitable Foundation for the benefit of underprivileged youth. While the major goal of the foundation was to provide funds to support existing programs in the Bay Area, it also created an innovative new experience: a series of winter-long 'Let's Go Play in the Snow' field trips.

THE END

CPSIA information can be obtained at www.ICGtesting.com
Printed in the USA
BVOW042202090912

299715BV00006B/28/P